TEACHER
IN MATT

"We have to d[...] gun."

"You're kidding. I've never even touched one."

"So what? Now you'll touch one. And by the way, is that your car parked out front? The red sports car?"

I smiled proudly. "Yes."

"Well, you'd better get rid of it. Too conspicuous for a detective. Get something, you know, brown. A sedan." I stared at him in stunned silence. "Now then"—Tito slid the notebook across to me, along with a file folder— "You'll start by reading it all. Make yourself comfortable. Sit on the couch."

I moved over to the brown-tweed sofa and opened the notebook. He hadn't done a lot on the case. He had interviewed a couple of teachers besides me. As for my own interview, Tito had added a notation at the end that said, "Scattered, seems pissed off or depressed, but a sharp cookie who cares. She may think of something later. Let her stew for a week. Recontact."

Scattered? Cookie? Let her stew? Well, I was damned if I was going to drive a brown sedan.

FOLLOWING JANE

by

Shelley Singer

A SIGNET BOOK

SIGNET
Published by the Penguin Group
Penguin Books USA Inc., 375 Hudson Street,
New York, New York 10014, U.S.A.
Penguin Books Ltd, 27 Wrights Lane,
London W8 5TZ, England
Penguin Books Australia Ltd, Ringwood,
Victoria, Australia
Penguin Books Canada Ltd, 10 Alcorn Avenue,
Toronto, Ontario, Canada M4V 3B2
Penguin Books (N.Z.) Ltd. 182-190 Wairau Road,
Auckland 10, New Zealand

Penguin Books Ltd, Registered Offices:
Harmondsworth, Middlesex, England

First published by Signet,
an imprint of New American Library,
a division of Penguin Books USA Inc.

First Printing, March 1993
10 9 8 7 6 5 4 3 2 1

PUBLISHER'S NOTE
This is a work of fiction. Names, characters, places, and incidents either
are the product of the author's imagination or are used fictitiously, and
any resemblance to actual persons, living or dead, events, or locales is
entirely coincidental.

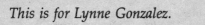

This is for Lynne Gonzalez.

The author wishes to thank Albert Smith and Dick Graham at Siegle's Guns in Oakland, Sergeant Jim Knudsen of the Alameda County Sheriff's Department, and Robin Blake at the Santa Cruz Beach Boardwalk.

Prologue

The screaming woman ran out of the cereal aisle, punctuating her first long cry with short, sharp, wordless shrieks as she knocked an elderly shopper to the floor, pushed her way past Jane, past the checkouts, and, clawing at the slow-opening electronic doors, out to the parking lot.

The clerks who didn't freeze quickly scattered, one heading after the screamer, another for the old man struggling to his feet. Jane stood, paralyzed, near a small clot of gaping customers, even when a cry from somewhere down the cereal aisle—"Oh my God! Get help!"—stirred some of the others to move in that direction.

She didn't move until Borden, the store manager, ran past her yelling "Man your registers! Stay at your posts!" and several cashiers turned back toward their checkouts. Jane wasn't working a register. It didn't matter if she abandoned the shopping carts she had just brought in from the parking lot. She could go and look. She hurried down the aisle behind her boss.

Several people were blocking her view, but she was able to see over the shoulder of the woman in front of her, and when the woman turned, lurching blindly, vomiting, away from the scene, Jane got an even better look at the man on the floor.

He was lying in blood and he wasn't moving. His white shorts weren't really white anymore. The floor around him was spattered and smeared with red, littered with cereal that had fallen from the broken, bloody scrap of box he still held in his hand. Her gaze circled and finally, before the tears blinded her, focused on the butcher knife that was planted in the middle of his chest. She began to sob.

The manager had shoved through to the body, and after ordering an employee to call the police, stood looking down at it. Then he turned his head and spoke to Jane.

"Isn't this someone you know?"

When she didn't answer she heard Mark speaking for her, from the small group huddled on the other side of the body.

"Yeah. William Anderson. He's one of our teachers."

Mark's voice sounded cold and flat. Jane rubbed her tears away and looked across at him. His face was rigid, until he met her eyes. Then his own eyes, and the lines of his mouth, softened, as if he might start crying, too.

1

I was lying on the couch dreaming my way through a disjointed student paper when the bark-alarm of Gilda's dogs, followed immediately by a loud knock on my own door, blasted me upright. I swung my legs off the couch and into the coffee table, tipping it over and spilling the rest of the papers onto the phony Persian rug along with a bowl of corn chips.

"Just a minute!" I yelled, taking off my reading glasses and glaring at the mess. I tied the old white terry-cloth robe more securely over my third-best underwear, stuck my feet into my sloppy loafers, and shuffled over to bang on the wall that connects my half of the duplex with Gilda's.

"Quiet in there, you guys!" The dogs barked once more and stopped.

I glanced at my imitation Swatch: 7:30. Gilda must be at one of her meetings. I looked out the front window. The man standing on the stoop was my age, somewhere around forty. He was short, maybe five-seven, and block-shaped. He was wearing a pale gray suit and a pale blue shirt, no tie. He looked like an ice cube.

He gazed back at me benignly, whipped out his wallet, flipped it open, and pointed at some kind of ID. I turned on the outside light to see it better; he held it closer to the glass. A private investigator's license. The face in the photo, square and pale, matched the one in the window. Neither one matched my fantasies of what a PI should look like.

So, I thought, the case has moved into the private sector.

"If you'll open the door on its chain," he said, "I'll pass the ID through so you can see it better." His voice was a deep, soft baritone, not what I had expected—no sharp edges, no ice.

I opened the door. He pulled the card out of his wallet and passed it through the narrow gap.

"Francis Broz," he said. Yes, that was the name on the card. "I hope I didn't wake you up." He eyed my outfit.

"I wasn't sleeping. I was working."

"Oh." He was not impressed. "I'd like to ask you some questions. I believe you teach at Berkeley Technical High School?"

I handed his ID back to him. "I'm sorry, Mr. Broz, I'd love to be able to help, but I don't know anything about William Anderson's death. I hardly knew him. The police questioned me once and found me useless."

He smiled a sweet smile, like a baby's. "I'm sure that's not true, but the fact is, I'm not exactly here about Anderson. I'm here about the disappearance of one of your students, Jane Wahlman her name is. Ran away or something. Five-six weeks ago.''

''You're trying to find Jane?''

His pale eyes studied me, taking in my surprise and my obvious interest.

''That would be my goal,'' he said.

I undid the chain and opened the door. ''Would you like a cup of coffee?''

''Yeah. I would. Thanks.''

He stepped in, glancing warily at the full suit of armor that stood against the entry wall, a pole-axe in its mailed fist. A gift from an ex-boyfriend, a museum curator. Unfortunately, I can't wear it. I'm five-nine. Its original owner—the knight, not the boyfriend—had been about five-two.

''A relative?'' he asked.

''Not that I know of.''

As we walked past the couch, his eyes slid over the mess of papers and corn chips on the floor and settled on my antique oak upright. ''Nice piano,'' he muttered.

''Thank you.'' It was an old beauty. The kind of piano that would be an heirloom if you were an heir, or had one.

He took a chair at the kitchen table and watched me measure the beans into the grinder, pour the coffee into the filter cone, turn on the flame under the kettle. His scrutiny made me uncomfortable, made me remember my uncombed hair, the snagged threads hanging off my tatty old robe. And the fact that under the robe, I was nearly naked.

''I'll just go get dressed while this is heating.''

"Sure. Go ahead."

By the time I returned to the kitchen, dressed in jeans, Birkenstocks, and a clean T-shirt, my hair combed, the kettle had begun to shriek; Broz was just turning off the burner. I made the coffee and brought two cups to the table.

"Your name is Broz?"

"Yeah. That's right. Francis."

"Sounds familiar. Would I have heard it before?"

He sipped at his coffee. "Josip. You're a history teacher, right?" He jerked his head toward the door to the living room, in reference, probably, to the metallic friend I call Ivanhoe. "Tito. Josip Broz. Of the former Yugoslavia. In fact that's what people call me. Tito."

I shrugged, feeling stupid. "Of course. Tito. I don't know where my mind is."

"I can see where you might be a little preoccupied. Anderson getting stabbed to death—and the cops not having a clue after almost two months—that must make the rest of you teachers kind of nervous."

"No," I said. "After all, it didn't happen at school."

At first I'd been horrified, along with everyone else, and maybe a little scared. But the week after the murder was Spring Break, and I'd gone off for a quiet few days in the Sierra, met a muscular ranger, and managed to put the whole thing out of my mind. When I got back to school, of course, people were still talking about it. But then Jane had taken off, and I had been more distressed by

that than by Anderson's murder. The police were
not. They mumbled around about her for a day
or so, shrugged a figurative shrug, and got right
back to chewing over the same old questions and
answers about Anderson. I thought their priori-
ties were questionable.

Broz nodded and made a note. "I guess that
would help, not happening at school."

"I thought we were going to talk about Jane
Wahlman."

"That's right, we are. And you were one of her
teachers."

"Senior World History. Yes."

"And you obviously care about her."

"Yes. I liked—like—her. She was one of my favorite students."

"Real smart, good student?"

"No, not at all. But she tried."

"What did you think when she disappeared?
You must know her pretty well."

"No. I don't." There are so many of them. But
what *had* I thought? I hadn't thought anything at
first, I'd just felt sad, and angry—she was one of
the good ones, and what the hell had happened
to her, anyway? When I'd finally gotten as far as
thinking, I'd thought she was old, at seventeen,
for running. I wondered if her presence at the
market the night of Anderson's murder had had
anything to do with it, if the ugliness of his death
might have kicked her over the line emotionally
from holding on to letting go. A line I hadn't
known she was walking.

Broz swallowed the last of the coffee in his cup and eyed the pot on the stove.

I poured more for both of us.

"So, why don't you tell me what you're thinking? Did you go along with the cops—that she was just your basic runaway?"

"I guess I did. There wasn't any reason to think anything else. It happens. Too often."

"And you've got her boyfriend, Mark Hanlon, in the same class, right?"

I nodded.

"So tell me about him. What's he like? Has he been acting different? Was he upset when she went missing?"

Missing. Disappeared. His choice of words worried me.

I put it to Broz directly. "You seem reluctant to call her a runaway. You think something worse has happened?"

He shook his head, sighing. "Sure she's a runaway. She took some of her clothes. Tell me about the boyfriend."

"The police don't do much about these cases, do they? The teenagers?"

"No. They figure they don't have time to chase down all the runaway kids. They don't. Tell me about the boyfriend."

I wasn't sure I was finished talking about the police, but I obliged. "Mark is a nice enough kid. He's been quieter since she left, and his grades have dropped. Is that what you want to know?"

"What kind of girl would you say Jane is?

Doesn't sound like she got in trouble or anything like that.''

"No. No trouble. She was pleasant to have in class. Bright enough. Quiet and sweet and likable. She didn't take a lot of energy and I didn't pay her a lot of attention. Not with thirty-five other kids in the same room, half of them acting like fools.'' Just saying it made me feel tired, made me think of the papers lying on the living room floor.

He nodded at me, serious and understanding. "One thing I wanted to ask you: What about her leaving so close to graduation, without her diploma? Doesn't that seem peculiar?''

It had at the time, I remembered, but you learn not to be too surprised at what kids do, and we'd all been so swept up in the murder investigation. "Yes, it does. But she might not have cared about the diploma. Some of them don't think it's worth anything. She was barely hanging on to a C-plus in History.''

"Ever meet her folks?''

"I don't think so. At least I don't remember meeting them.''

"Ever get any idea there might be a problem there?''

"After she left there was some talk among the teachers, of course. But nobody really knew anything. There were two runaways last year, at least three the year before. I saw her in school, that was all. You help them get through one class. If you wanted to do more than that you'd have to follow them around, follow them home.'' I felt like I was flunking an exam I badly wanted to pass, and the feeling was making me just a little snappish.

He raised his hands, palms up, placating. "What about her boyfriend—before she disappeared? What I mean is, was he acting funny? Pissed off? Did you see him with her, and if you did, how did they act? Did you ever hear him talk to his friends about her, or about how he was feeling? Before or after she left? Did they break up or have a fight?"

"Well, let me think." I gave it a good thirty seconds and came up with only vague impressions. "I remember seeing them together in the halls, at lunch, once or twice, maybe more, actually, and they just seemed like kids who were dating. I never heard they broke up, and I never saw them fight. I never watched that closely."

He drank some coffee, scratched his ear, stared at the table. "Okay, let's get off that for a while. What about the Anderson guy? How well did you know him?" He leaned toward me, eyes narrowed in a caricature of a squinting sleuth.

Anderson again? I had been sitting with my elbows on the table, holding my cup of coffee. I put the cup down and leaned closer to Broz, watching his face.

"You think his murder and her running off are connected?"

He sat back, waving the thought away like a fly. "Nah. Probably not. He was a teacher at her school. She worked at the market where he got killed. They're both locals, same territory. Obviously their paths had to cross from time to time. Doesn't mean much.''

"You *do* think there's a connection.'' Otherwise, why would he be asking about Anderson? "She was in his senior English class this year.''

"Yeah, but so were a lot of other kids, you know? Doesn't mean a thing.''

"Well, why not? I mean, it's certainly possible, isn't it? *That's* the angle you're following?''

He snorted. " 'Angle.' Jesus. No, I don't think the kid killed the teacher and took off—two weeks after she killed him, for Christ's sake!''

I hadn't said anything about Jane killing Anderson, I thought. Was that what he had in mind?

"Stop staring at me like that!'' he growled. "And stop getting carried away. Can't you just tell me what you know about the man? His friends? His family?''

For a moment I had a childish impulse to clam up, make him pay me in kind for anything I told him. But I didn't have anything to clam up about. "I didn't know Anderson well, and I didn't know his friends. I don't even know if he had any. He kept to himself. I met his wife at faculty parties once or twice. She seemed nice enough.''

"You didn't like him.''

"I don't know if I'd say that.'' He smirked, waiting. "Okay, maybe I didn't. But the man was murdered, for God's sake. He wasn't that bad.'' I hesitated. Broz nodded encouragingly. "He had this strong physical presence. Not attractive, not magnetic, but strong. He acted friendly, he even slapped an occasional back. He was always polite, even when he was lecturing people on flaws in their lifestyles. Smoking, drinking, eating, that kind of thing . . .''

Broz laughed. "Eating?''

I smiled at him, shaking my head. "You know the type. And when he made the effort to be friendly, he was too friendly. When he was polite, he was too polite. Nothing he did socially ever seemed real or comfortable. He didn't seem to be, you know, *with* the rest of the teachers. He kept himself apart. I never heard him talk about anything personal.''

He'd had a cold face, too: narrow, intelligent, unexpressive. I could see it clearly. More clearly than I could see Jane's. I hated that.

"What about students? Any problems with students?''

"Of course!'' The question was too ridiculous. "We all have problems with students. This is Berkeley Technical High we're talking about. The teachers call it Berkeley Pyrotech.''

Broz finished his coffee and stood up. I stood up, too. "Okay. I won't keep you any longer this evening. But would you do something for me?''

"Sure, if I can.''

"Think about it. Think about Jane Wahlman, about everything you ever saw or thought or heard about her. And let me get back to you in a few days. Okay?''

"Okay. You can reach me at school next week, then it's out for the summer. And here. I'm in the book.''

"Yeah, so am I.'' He handed me a business

card. "But here's my card anyway. And if you think of anything before I get back to you, call me. You'll probably have to leave a message, I'm in and out. Mostly out. Working on overload. You know how it is."

I walked with him to the living room, but he wasn't quite ready to leave. He stopped at the upright and played an arpeggio.

"You play?" he asked.

"Kind of. I'd like to. I've taken lessons twice. For a while when I was ten, and for a few months last year. I keep meaning to get back to it."

He was doing scales. "Great hobby. You ought to just do it." He stopped playing and shifted his focus to the top of the piano, to the silver-framed photograph of two very short, very round, blond, curly-haired, light-skinned, middle-aged people, standing in front of a canvas awning that said LAKE'S GROCERY.

"Who's that?"

"My parents."

He frowned at me. I have straight, dark brown hair. I'm not short. I'm thin, with olive-toned skin and a longer, straighter nose than either of the two people in the photo.

But all he said was, "Well, back to work. If you think of anything at all, please give me a call." Then he played a few skillful, slushy bars of "I'll Be Seeing You," patted the piano's turn-of-the-century soundbox, and strolled the rest of the way to the door.

2

I'm usually pretty good at using weekends to forget all the realities that won't leave me alone during the week.

I do a little shopping, a little puttering, and maybe, if it's absolutely necessary, a quick sweep-through of the house. Then I indulge in the self-hypnosis of TV sports, floating in limbo, looking back at nothing and forward only to whatever hot date the evening promises—should it promise such a thing.

That had been my plan for this Saturday, but I was having attention-span problems. I couldn't concentrate on the limbo at hand.

I went to the liquor store for beer and chips and to the natural foods market for their antidotes: a Rocky the Range Chicken, a nice piece of shark, unsprayed spinach, carrots and potatoes, fruit.

But when I got home and unpacked the bags, I realized that somewhere between the beer and the shark my mind had drifted back to the day before, a day that had been colored by my talk with Tito Broz, and, while so drifting, I'd forgotten half the things I'd meant to buy.

I wandered into the living room. There were last week's corn chips, under the couch and ground into the rug, the ones that had been calling out to the vermin of Berkeley since Thursday night. A brief foray with the vacuum cleaner and I was ready to lapse into perfect peace.

Which I did not find anywhere inside my head. Instead there were scenes from Friday's classroom, a conversation I'd had with another teacher, and, overlaying it all, a picture of Jane Wahlman. Her face, her pretty eyes—I didn't remember their color, of course, but they looked so damned sad!—kept intruding. The pale skin, the dark hair. Like Snow White. Had she eaten a bad apple?

I laid a fire in the smoke-smudged brick fireplace for later, when I brought my date back for a nightcap, and glanced around, satisfied with the way the place looked.

I then ruined the way it looked, but only temporarily, by rolling the TV table out of the bedroom and placing it at the end of the couch. Still a few minutes early.

When Jane had run off, or disappeared, or whatever we were going to call it, we'd heard that a missing persons report had been filed. The police asked a few questions around school: Any problems with her grades? Any changes in her behavior? I hadn't seen anything unusual, and as far as I knew, neither had anyone else. A lot of the kids get weird toward graduation, and this year they'd had the additional excitement and horror of Anderson's murder. Everyone, including the teachers and the cops, was caught up in that drama, and Jane had gotten lost in more ways than one.

Pro bowling was about to start. I grabbed a Granny Smith apple and flicked on the remote.

I scrutinized the two men going for the prize. Bowling is not one of my favorite spectator sports, but I prefer it to golf and car racing; pro golfers never look like anyone I would want to know, and all you ever see of race drivers during the competition is their cars. I prefer gladiators I can see and identify with.

One of the bowlers was medium-tall, thin with a tiny potbelly. He was wearing maroon pants and his hair was oiled and sculpted into a 1952 pompadour. The other was short and square, with a flat-top haircut, round little cheeks, and sane brown pants. He looked something like Tito Broz. He was my man.

For a while I was engrossed, until my man lost badly and was replaced by a challenger as unappealing as the winner.

I began to think about my encounter, the day before, with Rob Harwood.

I had just parked my car and was heading for class when I heard him call my name and turned to see him trotting across the parking lot, waving at me. I stopped just outside the school's main entrance and waited for him to catch up.

Rob is good-looking, thirty-five, blond, slender, short, always well dressed in a slick way, and very, very serious. We've never dated. He's never been any more interested in me than I am in him, and he had never trotted anywhere to be with me before.

"What's up, Rob?" I asked in a friendly fashion.

He jerked his head and his thumb, indicating that he wanted me to step to the side with him, out of the stream of traffic. I obliged.

"You got a visit from a private detective, a guy named Broz, didn't you?"

I nodded. "Last night."

"Me too. I was on my way out and didn't have time for more than a few words with him. He said he'd been talking to you. He wants to see me again. What's going on?" His tone was bright, interested.

"Just what he must have told you—he's looking for Jane Wahlman, questioning her teachers. I guess she was in one of your classes, too." He taught speech and sophomore English.

"Not a class. The drama club. The Mummers." Now that he'd mentioned it, I did recall Jane talking about the club once. I had thought at the time she seemed awfully quiet for an actor.

"Ah," I said meaninglessly.

"What kinds of questions did he ask you?"

I hadn't seen any reason not to tell Harwood about the conversation, so I did. He shook his head.

"Well, I don't know about you, but I wasn't very impressed with him."

"I like him. I think he's smart and interesting." I said it bluntly and with no inflection, wondering what Harwood was after.

"You do?" He stared at me, clearly surprised. Rob had his own ideas about what women found interesting in men. Several questions flickered across his face, but he didn't have the nerve to ask any of them. He wrinkled his fair brow. "Well, if you say so. Maybe we can talk more about this later. Got to run now."

He pushed open the door, held it until I was through, and glided off down the hall.

Was Harwood nervous about something, or just being a busybody?

We hadn't talked again, and the distance of a day's time hadn't made his motives any clearer to me.

I turned down the sound on the bowling show, went to the piano, and picked out "I'll Be Seeing You." If I were to take lessons again, would I practice? Aimlessly, I thumbed through some of the sheet music stacked on top, near the picture of my parents, standing in front of our store. Far away. Dead. Gone. A heart attack, a stroke, and the store—torched in the riot-fires of the Sixties, torn down with so much of the old Minneapolis North Side. God, how I missed them, missed myself as a child, sometimes, too. I hadn't always been a teacher. I had been Robin Hood, Ivanhoe, Nancy Drew.

I looked again at the TV. A horse race. Who cared?

I thought about Mark, sitting in class the day before, staring out the window, a depressed heap of long bones, choking on his vision of the future.

And all of them, world-weary, sophisticated Big

Kids. Even the ones who liked school were long gone, in their minds, from Berkeley Tech.

So I had pulled that old faker, Relevance, out of my bag of tricks—I use it sparingly because, as far as I'm concerned, nothing in history or about it is ever irrelevant—and gave them something to think about.

"Today," I told them, "We're going to talk about you. You as history."

"We ain't dead yet," Pissed-Off Purvis grunted from the back of the room. His real name is Gerald, but only teachers call him that.

"Living history," I said. "More or less." I paused for the much smaller laugh. "You've read a lot about the past. You have some idea of how things change and move. Think about your lives now, some of the things that have happened around you, the lives of your friends, people you know"—and what about their deaths? their disappearances? Would they say anything about that, I wondered—"the way the world is, the way you think it's going to be."

Mark sat slumped on his tailbone, scowling out the window, a tall, freckled boy with red-brown hair. At seventeen he had almost grown into his hands and feet, but sitting, his arms and legs never had enough room to unfold.

Jane's close friend, Lorene Johnson, was clutching a ballpoint in her caffè latte-colored hand, staring at her desk. Was either of them thinking of Jane?

"Let's hear some of your ideas. Mark?"

He looked up at me, startled, his face open.

I smiled at him. *It's a game, Mark. Play the game.*
"What's your place in history?"

Mark sighed and shrugged. He looked up at me,
the soft lines of his young face hardening.

"If I'm lucky," he said. "I won't have one."

A few nervous laughs, a few blank stares. I
glanced at Lorene. She was gazing at him, nodding thoughtfully.

"What do you mean, Mark?"

"People who have a place in history are mar-
tyrs, you know? Or big-time criminals. Or both.
They either mess up other people's lives or they
mess up their own. None of it makes any difference."

"Yeah," Lorene said. "Best you can do is have
a life, make a living. No statues, no electric chair."

"Come on, Lorene," I said. "You think the
world would be a better place if King and Gandhi
had been accountants?"

She laughed. "Oh, maybe they won a few little
things. But they both got killed, so what good did
it do them, anyway?"

"Yeah." Pissed-Off Purvis stretched his legs
into the aisle and stared at me, below face-level.
Whenever he talks to a female, student or teacher,
he talks to her breasts. Purvis is an amazingly pale
blond who never looks quite clean and has trouble talking without profanity, obscenity, or scat-
ological reference. I braced myself. "You gotta
take for yourself. Like those Mongolian guys. Nobody fucked with them." Good old Purvis, true
to form. The Mongol hordes would probably be
all he'd remember of world history. He got a few

hisses, a few laughs for his opinion, and several of the more strait-laced members of the class glared at him for his language. I had long since given up. It simply *was* his language.

Mark had turned back toward the window, a disgusted look on his face.

One of the more socially conscious girls snarled at Purvis, "What about the environment? What about crime?" Yes, I thought, that's right. What about murder, and what about kids who disappear?

Several hands were waving at me from around the room, but I wanted to hear from Jane's friends.

"So—what about those things? Mark? Lorene?"

Mark twisted around in his seat. "What about them? It's all too hard to control. There are too many variables. It's too complicated. . . ." His voice rose, wavered, choked off. He turned red, closed his mouth, faced the window again.

My own throat felt tight. I coughed to open it up, as though I were making some kind of statement.

"Should we just give in, then? Accept the bad things that happen? Accept violence and trouble?"

"Sometimes," Purvis said, "violence works out okay."

He got the attention of the whole class with that statement, and he made the most of it.

"Sometimes somebody kills a guy like Mr. Phony Anderson."

Shocked silence. Once again I was amazed at

the extent of Purvis's hostility—what had happened to this kid in seventeen short years?—and this time, I was also fascinated by it. I wanted to hear more. I took a deep breath—and the bell rang.

They all streamed out the door.

That had been my Friday, and it was ruining my Saturday.

The TV screen was displaying two young welterweights in the second round of battering each other. I like boxing. Good, direct action, no pie in the sky, no maybe-I-won, maybe-I-lost. I picked my favorite. In the blue trunks: Juan Orozco, a young stud from Central America who looked like someone I'd dated the year before.

I watched the fight. Orozco of the blue trunks was outboxing his opponent, jabbing again and again with a fast, wicked left. The other guy's knees buckled, but he got himself right again before the bell.

Good, direct action, yes, indeed. They grunted, sweated, danced, totally focused, alive, armored in muscle, absolutely in that ring. Simple goals, simple solutions.

Armored. I remembered the day Jane had brought in a book on medieval costumes to show me. I had told the class that medieval Europe was my favorite area of study, and she had remembered. She said she liked medieval history, too, because it was "like fairy tales." She couldn't have cared less about Canute, or Alfred, or William the Conqueror, or even Ethelred the Unready. It was Arthur, Guinevere, and Lancelot she loved. They were real, she insisted, the legend was real history, and Guinevere was her hero. I asked her if she'd ever read *Ivanhoe*, one of my personal favorites, and she had, but she dismissed it as "just a story," and said Ivanhoe was a jerk for not marrying Rebecca.

I thought she had something there.

Tito Broz's card was still on the end table, next to the phone, where I'd left it Thursday night. I picked it up, looked at it, dropped it back on the table, picked it up again, and dialed. The answering machine said that Francis Broz was out of the office. I left my name and number.

Orozco had his opponent on the ropes; good for him. The ref pulled them apart. I turned down the sound, still watching the screen, picked up the card again, and dialed a second time. This time I asked him to call me back as soon as possible. Juan landed a solid right to the jaw, the other guy fell. I turned the sound back up just in time to hear that Orozco was the new champ.

It was time to start thinking about getting ready for my date, who wasn't very much older than Juan. Our second date. His name was Charlie; he looked like a young Marlon Brando. I had been looking forward to this for days.

The phone rang.

"This is Tito Broz. You got something?"

"Not exactly." I hesitated. Dead silence at the other end. "Look, I'd just like to talk to you. I wonder if we could meet for dinner one night this week?"

He was silent again for a moment.

"I'm kind of busy right now. If you've got something about the kid . . ."

"I know you're busy. You mentioned that Thursday. But maybe I can help."

"Help?"

"Yes, help."

"You paying for this dinner?"

I laughed. "Yes, I'm paying for this dinner. And I'll try to make it less of an ordeal than you seem to think it's going to be."

He laughed, too. "Okay. I like Szechuan food." He named a restaurant on University Avenue. "Make it tonight at seven."

3

"I like this outfit better than the bathrobe," Tito Broz said. "Better than the T-shirt, too."

Well, I thought, if I had to trade in an evening with Charlie for one with Tito Broz, I'm at least glad my version of the power tie is being appreciated. Black high-top pants, blue jacket with detachable shoulder pads—attached—white silk blouse, black Romika shoes, and a pair of black-and-silver earrings that look like part of the interior of an art deco theater.

But I didn't want him to get into the habit of grading me on my wardrobe. I raised a cool eyebrow.

"You're wearing exactly what you were wearing Thursday."

"Sure." He laughed. "I haven't been home. You want a beer? I'll buy you a beer."

I must have been more nervous than I thought, because I actually dithered internally about that simple question. Was the deal good only for beer? Did I want wine? If I asked for wine would he think I was a wimp? I got a grip on myself, and stopped thinking like one. This was California. I had seen sixty-year-old union members with face stubble and potbellies drinking white wine in neighborhood saloons. And I didn't want wine anyway.

"Thanks. Beer sounds good."

He ordered Tsing Tao. "That okay?"

"Fine."

We studied our menus.

"How about something with seafood and something with chicken?" I asked.

"Sure." The waiter returned with our beers, we ordered, and I watched Tito pour carefully, nearly foamlessly, into his glass.

"So," he said, "I brought my brains. Pick away."

"I'm not sure what I want to know."

"You want to know who killed Anderson and what happened to Jane Wahlman. Admit it."

"Well, that, yes." I had a sudden moment of panic. Has he already solved it? I wondered. He wouldn't need my help if he'd already solved it. "But what I really want to know is what it's like being a private investigator."

He nodded and smiled. "You're writing a book, right?"

"No."

He gazed at me for a moment, looked thoughtful, and said, very seriously, "It's a hell of a lot of fun."

"That's not what I expected to hear," I said, laughing.

"I was supposed to say, 'Hey, it's a job like any other job. Lots of times it's boring. Most of the work is repetitive and tedious.' " He grinned. "That's all probably true. But all jobs stink in some ways. I'm self-employed so I love the boss, and what can I say? The work's more fun than anything else I can think of to do. I get to act tough and in-charge, carry a gun, meet a lot of weird people, and use my head to solve cases. Doesn't that sound like fun to you?"

"God, yes." Maybe not the part about the gun.

"You say that with a lot of feeling." Now he was looking at me sidelong, suspiciously. Our dinner arrived, along with a pot of tea. He dug right in. Sure, what did he have to worry about? He wasn't applying for a job.

"Look, Tito, you said yourself you were over-loaded with work. I've got the whole summer free. I've got some ideas"—I didn't, but that was all right—"about Jane Wahlman. I'm smart, you know that. And I'm strong."

He pointed a sauce-coated chopstick at me. "You're pretty skinny."

"But I'm fairly tall. I'll work hard and I'll work for nothing."

"You're skinny and you're tall. You don't look like your parents."

"I'm adopted."

"Ever find out anything about your back-ground?"

"Not much. My parents—the Lakes that is—were told that there's some Chippewa, some French, some Swedish. Not strange for someone who was born in Minnesota. And I'm Jewish by adoption."

"Lake?"

"Lakoff, before Ellis Island."

He grunted and shoved another chopstick-load of chicken and rice into his mouth. "Where'd you get a name like Barrett?"

"It's a lake in Minnesota. Barrett Lake."

He didn't laugh. People often do. "So you grew up out there?"

"Minneapolis."

"So all you know is you're a Jewish French Indian Swede named for a lake in Minnesota? That's it? You never tried to find out more?" He was pointing that damned chopstick at me again. "You've got a mystery of your own you never solved. Why do you want to solve the one I'm working on?"

"Because I know more about it than I know about my own." I could tell by his expression that he knew this was a bullshit answer. The truth was, I wasn't sure I wanted to find out the answers to my own mystery. Being an adopted princess had been pretty nice. "Besides, that's me, this is someone else. Look, I feel bad about Jane Wahlman, that I didn't somehow know to help her. That I didn't see her trouble in her face. There have been too many faces." He sighed. I continued anyway. "I'm not making a difference."

"Oh, great, a woman with a mission. And I thought that suit of armor by your door was only a decoration."

"It keeps out burglars. Listen, I'd just like to see something come out right. Fix something. Help you fix it."

He poured some tea into our cups. "Did it make you feel like an outsider, being adopted?"

"No. Well, maybe a little. Yes, sometimes." What the hell was he asking?

"That could be good. Outsiders make good observers. But what if it gets dangerous?"

"I'm not afraid." I hadn't been afraid at the store, even though my parents sometimes were, as the neighborhood got rougher and rougher and the violence came closer to us. "If I were afraid I'd be teaching in Walnut Creek, not Berkeley."

"It can be boring. And I'd make you do all the boring parts."

This was beginning to sound promising.

"Fine. What do I have to do to qualify as a private investigator?"

"To get a license you have to do a lot. But you don't need a license to work for someone who's got one. Like me. You work under my license."

I pushed my picked-at dinner aside and leaned forward.

"Do I? Work under your license?"

He poured more tea. "I don't think so. I'd have to spend a lot of hours teaching you. By the time you knew anything it would be fall and you'd be going back to school."

"I could take a lot off your shoulders. I learn fast. You'd save time in the end."

He sighed. "There's two more cases I need to work on. I should have turned one of them down. But I thought teachers liked to travel in the summer."

He was grasping at straws. I almost had him.

"I was going to take a cruise to Alaska. I'd rather do this. Listen, Tito, give me two weeks. If I'm not helping you enough by then, I'll go to Alaska."

"Ah, shit, Barrett—what do people call you, anyway?—I don't want to have to worry about someone else."

"They call me Barrett. And don't worry. Relax and enjoy it."

He burst out laughing. "Let me think about it."

"What do you have to lose?"

"The client. The case."

"If you're as busy as you say you are, you don't need this case anyway."

"You're a steamroller, you know that?"

"Actually, I'd forgotten." It was true. I'd almost forgotten, anyway. "I'll take the ball and run with it."

"Nose to the grindstone?"

"Fingers to the bone."

"Maybe you better tell me why you're so hot to 'fix' things. I don't trust missionary types."

"There are no Jewish missionaries." We both laughed at that. "So here's the story. I grew up in a grocery store at the low end of a great old neighborhood that was beginning to go bad. It was scary and it was ugly. A lot of kids my age were getting in trouble, people were racing to the suburbs to get away from the violence and the crime. But we had the store. We stayed.

"And I adapted by having fantasies—fantasies of being a superhero and fixing it all, sailing into the bad guys with a sword, shooting my bow and arrow and making everything right. But my parents were Old Country, and they convinced me that girls didn't do that kind of thing for a living, that if I wanted to help people I could help by teaching the children." I paused. He sat silent, watching me.

"You know what? I can't. Not ever enough. Not ever enough to make *me* feel good. And it makes me tired and frustrated and I want to goddammit *do* something about something before I explode or drop into a permanent stupor!"

He nodded, slowly, and took a healthy swallow of beer.

"That's all pretty general. Can you be more specific?"

"Son of a bitch," I muttered. He laughed. "All right, I'll get specific. I liked Jane but I didn't pay much attention to her. I didn't like Anderson, I don't know if anyone did. But everybody's been carrying on about his murder and ignoring her trouble—the police, the teachers . . . me, too. Yes, I feel guilty!" He nodded. "I don't know if it's because she's a girl or because she's a kid, or just because we know Anderson's dead and murdered and she's just another runaway. And then you show up. You're looking for her. Finally someone's noticed."

I shrugged. I had run out of words. I wasn't about to tell him about Guinevere and Rebecca, Arthur, Lancelot, and Ivanhoe.

"Okay. Now eat your dinner. You need the

weight. And tomorrow, eat a big breakfast and meet me in the office at nine A.M.''

Driving home, I began to realize just how good this Broz guy was. He now knew a lot more about me than I knew about him.

4

My landlady, Gilda, was on her knees weeding her herb border, when I stepped out the door the next morning on my way to Tito's office. Her dogs, Frantic and Harvey, were lying near her and assorted cats were weaving about, including a black-and-white kitten I'd never seen before. Gilda is a rescuer. I mean, she really does it. Finds foster homes for strays, that kind of thing.

She got to her feet, gracefully for a sixty-five-year-old, brushing some leaves off her Gray Panthers sweatshirt, the one that matches almost exactly the color of the long gray braid that hangs down her back.

"This is Franklin," she said, pointing at the kitten. "He needs a home."

"I'll ask around," I said quickly.

She shook her head. "I'm not pushing, Barrett. Henry was a great cat. But you can't mourn forever."

I'd lived with Henry for seventeen years. He'd been dead for two. "Mourning forever is one of the things I do best." Not to mention avoiding the consequences of Gilda's good works. I added, "And I'm going to be awfully busy."

"Doing something fun, I hope—and where are you going so early on a Sunday?"

I checked my watch. I had a few minutes. Quickly, I told her.

"That's wonderful!" she crowed. "First the car, now this!"

She was referring to the car I'd bought several months before, the week of my fortieth birthday. The red sports car parked at the curb. She'd been ecstatic, and I'd been pretty happy myself, when I'd broken the Sensible Transportation habit and gone for the five-year-old Mazda RX7 with the moon roof, the stereo, the new paint, and sixty thousand miles.

It was exactly what I'd been looking for. I bought it on the spot, flipping the bird at Time and Mortality.

And I had done all that before I'd even met Tito Broz.

"I didn't have any choice," I said. "Once I bought the car I *had* to become a private detective."

She laughed. "Absolutely. Now, tell me: Can I help?"

I told her truthfully that I didn't know enough, yet, to know if she could help. After we agreed to try to get together for a movie or something during the week, I took off for my day of instruction.

was right on time, but only because I'd driven the block repeatedly until 8:59.

ffice was over a futon shop on Telegraph uth Berkeley, just past the Oakland line. The stairs, lighted by two ancient wall sconces and a skylight, were steep and only fairly clean. The solid door at the top of the stairs bore a wooden plaque, held on by four brass-headed screws, that said FRANK BROZ, INVESTIGATIONS.

I knocked, heard his clear, deep, "Come on in," and turned the knob. He was standing near the window, looking out, and he was just hanging up the phone.

"That was the client. He wants to meet you."

This Tito Broz, I thought, is not a man who wastes time. Here I'd been a detective for, what? Two minutes? And I was already dealing with clients. Very flattering, but I had thought I'd get a chance to flop around in the shallows before he asked me to swim the Golden Gate. Apparently he was going to push me off the bridge at the south tower.

"Now?"

"Stop staring at me. Sit down and take it easy." I took a chair at the side of his desk. "I'll get you some coffee." He got up and crossed the room to a coffeemaker perched on top of a small, apartment-size refrigerator, poured two cups of coffee, put them on a tray with a carton of milk and a sugar bowl, and carried the tray back to his desk. The man really was a mass of surprises: I would never have expected him to own a serving tray and a sugar bowl.

"I'm not sending you over there today," he said. "You're not ready."

"Oh, all right." I guess I didn't sound disappointed enough, because he shook his head at me.

"You know," he said, pouring milk into his cup, "that's the trouble with women."

I felt the muscles in my face and chest go tight. "Oh? And what is that? What exactly is the trouble with women?"

"That's better," he said, smiling. "Get the blood flowing. What's the matter with women is no self-confidence." I started to speak but he held up a hand. "I'm not talking about native ability, but about conditioning. You aren't taught to bull-shit your way through life like men are. Most of you just don't have the right weapons to survive. Even if a guy has doubts, he knows enough to act like he doesn't, to act like he's right on top of it all. You gotta learn that. It's a bullshit world. The guy who wins is the guy who shovels faster. Or the woman. In the big world. Business. This business in particular."

I tasted the coffee. It was perfect. My mouth still felt tight. I sipped again. Maybe he had a point. Maybe. I would have to think about it. I was willing to learn. But not to be patronized. It wasn't as if I'd ever lived in a cocoon.

"Maybe I'll feel more confident when I have just the smallest idea of what if is I'm supposed to be doing."

He shook his head. "See, that's what I mean. You gotta pretend you're an old hand, for Christ's sake. Especially when you meet the client. Because he thinks you are."

"And when am I supposed to meet the client?" I could be ready in three or four days, I thought. I really do learn fast.

"Tomorrow night, at his house. But he can't make it until nine-thirty. That okay?"

Well, I would just have to learn faster. "Where does he live?"

"Berkeley Hills. I'll write out the address. And the directions. And stop worrying. We'll spend today getting you ready. Teaching you something about the business, how to deal with the people. By the time you meet the guy, you'll be moving on the case already and you'll be way ahead of him."

I tried to stop worrying. "Why does he want to meet me? Does he want me to go and visit him just so he can introduce himself? Or does he have something he wants to tell me about the case?"

"He wants to meet you so he can make sure the case is being 'handled competently.' Those are his words. Not mine." I opened my mouth to object, but Tito held up his hand. "See, what it is, he wanted me to work on this one case full-time, but he wouldn't, or couldn't, pay the price for it. I told him, 'Don't worry, I'm on it three-quarters, and I got an assistant on it full-time.' He wasn't happy, but he said okay, and he wanted to meet you, talk a little. I said you wanted to talk to him, too."

"Of course I do. But not with a resumé in my hand."

"No resumé. I already lied about your background. He thinks you were a cop. I didn't tell him where because he might check it out. I said I worked for him, but you work for me. He took that okay. So, today's class-time. We'll go over some stuff about interrogation and procedure, because you're going to be talking to him about finding his daughter and he's going to be checking you out.

"When you're asking him a question, you look at him like you can read his mind. Don't fill up the holes he leaves in the conversation. Give him time to do it. When you're answering, don't answer fast. Think. Take your time. Be smart, but be nice. And remember, I may not need this case, but without it, I don't need you. Oh yeah, before I forget. Remember to remind me we have to do something about getting you a gun."

"You're kidding. I've never even touched one." And I wasn't at all sure I ever wanted to.

"So what? Now you'll touch one. And by the way, is that your car parked out front? The red one?"

I smiled proudly, remembering my conversation with Gilda. "Yes."

"Well, you better get rid of it. Too conspicuous for a detective. They'd all see you coming a mile away. Get something, you know, brown. A sedan." I stared at him in stunned silence. "Now then . . ." He reached in his pocket and pulled out a wallet and a notebook. He extracted a photo of Jane from the wallet. It looked like a yearbook photo. "You'll need this when you're looking where people don't know her. Get a copy made for me. And here's my notes, and a folder of other stuff." He slid the notebook across to me, along with a file folder that had been lying on the desk. You'll start by reading it all. It won't be hard because I haven't done a whole hell of a lot yet. Make yourself comfortable. Sit on the couch. Toilet's down the hall on your right.''

I moved over to the brown tweed sofa, a foldout sleeper, I thought. I put the photo in my own wallet, and opened the folder. It contained clippings and notes about Anderson's murder on April 8—I'd forgotten that the weapon, a butcher knife, had apparently been picked up on the spot in the store's housewares department. There was a note on the autopsy. Anderson had been stabbed over and over again, both before and after the killing wound to the heart.

I opened the notebook. The first line told me that Jane had disappeared April 21. Tito's handwriting was small and slanted. Did that mean he was intelligent and emotional or fastidious and neurotic? I couldn't remember. I hadn't read a book on graphology since the Sixties. He moved around the office while I read, opening and shutting file drawers, whistling, drinking coffee.

The office was small—a second door led to what could be a closet or another room—but bright and airy, with three big windows. I wondered if he would give me a desk; there was only his, now, and two chairs, and the couch with an end table and lamp. If there was another room I could work there. Or we could move a second desk into this one. Or maybe I wouldn't be sitting very much.

What he had said was true. He hadn't done a lot. He had talked to the client, who was the missing girl's father, long divorced from the mother. He'd talked briefly to the mother, who was now also divorced from a second husband, and had written that he felt there was a lot more to find out from her, that maybe there was something "funny" about the second divorce. He had called, but had not yet seen, both Mark and Lorene, and had interviewed a couple of teachers besides me— he had not yet managed to get back to Rob Harwood. As for the notes from my own interview, which were short and somewhat barren, Tito had added a notation at the end that read, "Scattered. Seems pissed off or depressed, but a sharp cookie who cares. She may think of something later. Let her stew for a week. Recontact."

Scattered? Cookie? Let her stew? Well, I was damned if I was going to drive a brown sedan.

5

Tito and I had agreed on one thing—the place to start my quest was on Jane's home ground. First, her actual home. I would talk to her mother, see how she and Jane had lived. Study Jane's room. Look through her things.

Talk to her mother? I was uncomfortable about that. I would not find it easy to ask her some of the questions Tito said needed to be asked, questions that might multiply her nightmares: Excuse me for wondering, Mrs. Wahlman, but did your daughter give away all her most valued possessions before she disappeared? No, no, of course that doesn't necessarily mean she's jumped off a cliff. . . .

Then her friends, people she knew at school. And of course her job, which also happened to be a murder scene.

I was pretty busy during the morning, but I tried calling Jane's mother several times. She wasn't home and had no answering machine.

During my free period, I spent some time in the school office with the students' records.

Jane's were, mostly, as unremarkable as I had

expected them to be. Except for her potential. According to the various tests she'd been subjected to, including the Stanford-Binet, her intelligence was superior. Yet her schoolwork was only slightly better than average. She barely made it through in math and science, and had always pulled C's in History. She did her best work in English, and didn't seem to bother much with anything else. She had been an active member of the drama club since the beginning of her junior year.

Mark's records showed an average intelligence but he had worked hard enough to do well in school. Lorene was as bright as Jane but generally got better grades.

As long as I was sneaking around in private lives, I looked up Pissed-off Purvis—not because I thought he had anything to do with the case but because I was curious about him. His smarts and his grades matched, both barely elevating him to semi-civilized status. He had no extracurricular activities. Poor kid, I thought briefly. Briefly, because I'm no hypocrite—I hope—and I can't stand him.

Jane, as I already knew, lived with her divorced mother. So did Mark. Lorene's guardian was her grandmother. Purvis? An uncle.

"Find what you want?" Olivia, the school records clerk, who was not supposed to look over my shoulder, was looking over my shoulder as I finished writing down the names of some of Jane's teachers.

"Yes, thanks." I gave additional thanks, to the

Unknown, that word of what I was doing had not yet gotten around school. Olivia would have harassed me with questions I didn't have time for.

On the way back to my classroom, I picked up a copy of the yearbook and spent a few minutes at my desk checking out Jane's public persona.

She didn't have much of one. I had been right about the photo Tito had given me. It was her yearbook picture. And underneath it, where they list activities, there was only one—The Mummer's Club. I thumbed through to the Clubs section. Several good shots of Rob Harwood directing, I noticed. Jane was in the group photo, kneeling down in front, smiling. And she was in two of the scenes from plays, but in the background, not in the leads.

I still had five minutes before class, so I went to see Rob Harwood.

I opened the door of his classroom a few inches and peered in. He was standing at the chalkboard, pointing at a list of the parts of speech. Startled by the sound of the door opening, he turned to face me and frowned, clearly not pleased by the interruption. He told his class to look something up and came out into the hall, closing the door behind him.

"Sorry to bother you in the middle of a class, Rob, but I wanted to be sure I caught you today."

"Oh, that's all right, Barrett," he said blandly. "What's up?"

"I think you might know Jane Wahlman better than any of her teachers, maybe better than a lot of people, and I want to talk to you about her."

"Why?" He glanced nervously toward the door of his silent classroom.

"Because I'm working with Tito Broz—you know, the investigator who's trying to find her?"

He gave me a sidelong look, the kind of look people give to those who are not normal and possibly dangerous.

"Really." I handed him one of Tito's cards with my name scribbled at the bottom. "Kind of a summer job," I added lamely. Harwood nodded, still giving me the fish eye. I got mad.

"Listen, what's so damned strange about me working with a private investigator?"

"Nothing, Barrett. Sorry. I was just a little surprised. I mean . . ." Good. Truculence had convinced him. He believed me.

"How about having lunch with me today and discussing it?"

"Oh, I'm afraid I'm busy today. Of course I'd like to help if I can—although I don't know how I can. But maybe in a couple of days? Somewhere away from school?"

At my questioning look he added, "We don't know what happened to her. And Jane is such a wonderful girl, so sensitive. It doesn't seem right to be talking about her where people who knew her—know her—might overhear. All right?" He smiled and ducked back inside his classroom, closing the door softly in my face.

"All right," I said to the closed door. The bell was about to ring. Time to get back to my own classroom.

Right at lunchtime Tito marched in the door—

I'd given him a copy of my schedule for the week—carrying a greasy paper sack in one hand and an airline bag in the other.

"Free for lunch?

I nodded and pointed at the paper bag. "Is that it?"

"Yeah. Burgers. Good ones." He pulled a wad of paper napkins out of his pocket.

"And what's in there?" I glanced at the airline bag now sitting next to my desk.

"Underwear, toothbrush, shirt, you know. I'm going to LA."

I opened my mouth to protest, but he kept on talking.

"We got a tip. On the phone machine. Man, woman, I couldn't tell. Whoever it was used this weird squeaky voice. Said that Jane was in LA with some cousin of hers. Could be bullshit. Keep doing what you're doing. I won't be gone more than a day or two. I'll stay in touch. Here, eat your burger."

The burgers were huge. He'd brought fries, too.

"This food will kill us both," I told him.

"I couldn't find any tofu. Eat as much as you can."

We talked about my plans for the day while I ate all of my burger and a few fries, and he ate everything else. Then he tidied up my desk, packed all the debris back in the paper bag, said good-bye, and walked out the way he'd come in, a bag in each hand.

So I'm on my own for a while, I told myself. So what? In fact, so much the better. Sink or swim.

Yes, indeed. I would just proceed as if he were not going to find her in LA. In fact, I admitted guiltily to myself, I didn't want him to. I wanted to do it. I would not let Jane suffer from my inexperience. I'd turn the case over to Tito entirely if I thought that was happening. But the more I thought about it, the better I liked the idea of jumping aggressively into the case all by myself, making my own mistakes and my own discoveries. I could feel the adrenaline pumping. The chase was on.

Maybe it was that enormous lump of meat Tito had fed me.

I was ready for Lorene when she arrived for senior World History. "Could I talk to you for a second?"

The tall young woman nodded solemnly and stopped beside my desk.

"You're a good friend of Jane's, right?"

"Yes, I am." She spoke emphatically.

"I wonder if you could find some time in the next day or so to meet with me. I want to talk to you about her."

She looked surprised. "What for?"

"Could we talk about that when we meet?" The room was filling up.

"I don't know . . ."

"I'm working with an investigator named Broz—I know he's already called you. When's a good time? After school? Tonight? Around seven-thirty or eight at your house?" Not too late—I had that appointment with the client at 9:30.

"Well, I guess so," she said again, looking at me doubtfully and taking her seat.

I meant to stop Mark on his way out but got waylaid by another student who wanted something signed. I would just have to catch him later.

It was two o'clock before I finally reached Jane's mother. At my request for a visit she sighed, hesitated, and, finally, agreed to talk to me at four o'clock, which gave me an hour to fill right after school. Not much time, but I had a couple of ideas.

At the end of the school day I shoved some left-over paperwork into my desk and raced out to my car. Parked under a tree on the lot, the RX7 looked shiny, sleek, and ready for work.

I slid into the driver's seat, snapped the catch on the moon roof, rolled down the windows, turned the key, and got that first blast of stereo sound from KJAZ—somebody's very cool version of "What's New" from the late Fifties or early Sixties.

In ten minutes I was pulling into the Solano Avenue parking lot of the SaveMor, where Jane had worked and where William Anderson had died. The lot was full of middle-aged Volvos, new BMWs, Mercedes of various models and ages, and VW bugs left over from the Sixties.

I thought of the market as the intersection of the case, where the death crossed the disappearance in either very odd synchronicity or cause and effect. I had read Tito's "folder of other stuff" on Anderson's murder carefully, along with his skimpy notes about Jane, and while I didn't have much time to stop, I thought I could at least poke around a little.

I walked in and asked the first employee I saw where I might find the manager. She pointed to a red-faced man with dark hair who was at that moment walking out the door. I ran after him and introduced myself. He smiled, nodded, and said his name was Floyd Borden.

"I'm afraid I can't stop and talk to you now," he said. "I was just on my way to pay a call on a wholesaler who keeps messing up our orders— you know how it is, nobody does anything right anymore."

"Isn't that the truth," I said. "Why don't I just walk along with you for a moment?"

"Well, I'm sure I can't imagine anything more delightful." He smiled, nodded, and licked his red lips, which were already wet.

The man was making me sick, but I smiled graciously. "Perhaps I can make an appointment to come and have a longer talk with you tomorrow? Perhaps then you could give me a tour of the store and tell me all about what happened the night that poor man died?" I was also making myself a little sick.

"That would surely be my pleasure," he said, smiling and nodding, his red face turning a little redder as he gazed at me.

"This is my car, right here." He stopped at a large, newish Cadillac. "Greatest cars in the world. What do you drive?"

I waved in the direction of my car, parked just a row away. "That red RX7 over there."

"That's a fine car, too. Maybe you'd like to take me for a ride in it over to the wholesaler? That way I could answer your questions and get my business done, all at once."

"I have another appointment," I told him, looking at my watch. "I was just hoping to catch you on the way. . . ."

"Oh, we'll need to have a longer talk than this. You're really working as a private eye? Excuse me for saying it, but you don't look like one."

"Yes I do," I said rather shortly. He laughed, smiled, nodded, and held up his hands as if to fend off a blow.

"Well, you want to know about Jane, or you want to know about the dead man?"

"How much time can you give me?"

"Five minutes today, as much as you need tomorrow."

Five minutes turned out to be just long enough for him to give me a very gory description of the last appearance of William Anderson.

"Blood all over the damned place—listen, I got to get going. You come by tomorrow, hear? Give me a call and come on by."

"I will. By the way, is Mark Hanlon on duty now?"

"Naw. Day off."

So much for killing two birds with one stone— or even one.

I said good-bye to Floyd Borden and, with time to spare, drove slowly to my meeting with Jane Wahlman's mother.

6

Roberta Clapton—she was still using her second husband's name—lived in northwest Berkeley, in a lower-middle-class neighborhood that ran about equal parts black, white, and brown, blue-collar, low-level white collar, and U.C. Berkeley student. The area was one short step below my own economically: a bit poorer, the houses slightly smaller and less pampered.

All in all a reasonably safe few blocks, with only the occasional burglaries that all East Bay neighborhoods live with.

I found a parking spot close to the right address, turned off the engine, pulled out my new pocket-sized notebook, and reread the questions I'd prepared. I made a couple of quick notes and stuck the book back in my pocket. There were few large trees on the block, none with a parking place under it, and the sun was summer-hot, so I propped the cardboard accordion-pleated sunshade up against the windshield before I locked up and got out of the car.

The address was 1512B. The main house, 1512, was a pale blue, paint-starved stucco bungalow with sheer curtains in the smudged front windows. To its right was a side gate of rickety one-by-fours, one of them broken, painted peachy-cream many years before. Through the overgrown side yard, I could just make out a smaller building at the back of the lot. With some trouble, I separated the gate's hook from its I-bolt, and, hooking it again behind me, negotiated the broken and uneven walk to the cottage.

The occupant of 1512B maintained her part of the property very well. The royal blue trim on the shingled cottage had been painted within living memory; the cedar shingles were gray with age, but they all seemed to be there and in good condition. The stairs were swept clean, and when I stepped up on the tiny front porch I noticed that the curtains were the same blue as the trim. Very neat. Neater, actually, than I like. I knocked, and waited.

One, two, three, four, five, six beats passed before the footsteps, another five before a voice asked who was there. Two more beats before the door opened. I wondered if she was old, or possibly disabled, to move so slowly.

She was neither. She was a small, pretty blonde of forty or so, with round hips and a small waistline, the kind of woman who can wear happily whatever tight pants current fashion calls for. I'm fairly pleased with myself the way I am, but I have always wondered how life would be different if I looked like a doll. This doll wore a slight frown.

I smiled. "It was nice of you to see me on such short notice."

"Oh, that's all right," Roberta Clapton spoke wearily. All right? I thought. Just all right? "Lucky you caught me on my day off." I followed her slow steps into the small house, trying to stifle the prick of dislike her words had caused. "All right," indeed. If *I* had a missing daughter I'd see anyone anytime, with no notice at all, if I thought it would help bring her back.

But I wasn't being fair. Why was I so eager to be critical? All I really knew at this point was that this woman was worn out, and not particularly happy to see me. And tidy.

The tiny living room was stuffed with overlarge furniture: a six-foot couch, a bulky tweed recliner, a big easy chair, several end tables, and a four-foot coffee table, all placed very precisely in their appointed spaces. The colors were all pastels: pale blue, pale green, pale yellow, bits of pink and white. She invited me to sit in the recliner.

"Can I get you anything? Any coffee?"

"No, thanks."

With a little smile—brave? grateful?—she sank down in the middle of the couch. "Where do you want to start?"

"I want to start with what you think might have happened to Jane. Do you think she ran away or . . . what?" Oh, wonderful. "Or what." I was going to have to get tougher if I wanted to do this. Someday I might have to use a word like "murdered" or "kidnapped," even with the mother of a victim.

"I don't know what happened to her. I suppose she just ran away." Then, as though it were an afterthought: "I hope that's all that happened. But in this world . . ." She sighed. "Anyway, I suppose it would be good to know. I suppose I'm glad that Janie's father hired Mr. Broz." Her mouth twisted downward. "I certainly don't have the money."

"How does Jane feel about her father? Does she see him often?" I thought it wouldn't hurt to go to my interview with the client that evening knowing a few things about him.

Clapton shrugged. "He gave her presents sometimes. She saw him once in a while."

"But how does she feel about him?"

"What do you want to know that for?"

Tidy, exhausted, and irritable. Maybe it was all right for me not to like her.

"Let me see if I can explain. I'm trying to learn to understand Jane. I need to learn everything I can about the people and places she knew. So I can find out what happened and where she is."

She sighed again. "I'm sorry. I didn't mean to grump at you. How does she feel about her father? Well. It's never easy to say how Jane feels about anything. I think she admires him, but she gets upset with him sometimes, too, because he has another family."

"What do you mean, 'It's never easy to say how Jane feels'?"

"Maybe it is for someone else. We weren't close."

"Can you tell me more? About your not being close?"

"We just weren't, that's all."

I would have to get back to that.

"And then there's a stepfather, isn't there?"

Her face went blank. "Yes."

I looked around the crowded little room. "And he lived here with you?"

"No. We lived together in the front house. And not for several years now." The woman's mouth snapped shut on the word "now," as if she were imprisoning the sentence she'd spoken. She looked away, her eyes vacant. I'd hit a nerve. What had the man done to her? Had he beaten her? And Jane? But this was not the empty, defeated look of the battered; it was the deliberately blank look of someone who doesn't want to show her feelings and would like to just damned well drop the subject, *now*.

Tito was right. There was something under the rug here that made an ugly bump.

"How close was Jane to her stepfather? Is she close to him now?"

She couldn't hold the vacant look. Fear, anger and something else—disgust—shot to the surface of her eyes.

"That's a funny way to put it," she said, harshly.

I was beginning to get an idea about that ugly bump. "I don't know what you mean, Mrs. Clapton."

"I'm sure you do know. I'm sure someone told you. And probably blamed me, too."

"I haven't talked to anyone else yet. I really don't understand."

"About Neil Clapton? And why I threw him out?"

I shook my head and waited.

"I think I do want some coffee. You sure you don't want some?"

"Positive, thanks." She fled the room and I was left alone to come to my own conclusions. A small, dull headache settled between my eyes. I rubbed my forehead.

Mrs. Clapton returned quickly with her coffee. She sat down abruptly and started to speak, in what sounded like the middle of a sentence begun in her own thoughts in the kitchen.

"The hard part was that she'd told a teacher, back when she was ten. The teacher called all three of us in. Neil—Mr. Clapton—said Janie was just mad at him because he'd had to punish her for not cleaning up her room. I remembered that, that he had punished her for not cleaning up her room. No dinner. So I said yes, he had punished her, just the week before she told this teacher. Neil kept at Janie until she finally said she was lying. She cried when she said it, but I thought, well, it's hard on a child to admit lying in front of three adults, isn't it? Lying about such a terrible, nasty thing? And of course, she'd have to be punished for lying."

"I see. He'd been abusing her. Sexually."

Mrs. Clapton didn't respond. She didn't look at me. "You have to understand, Janie and I weren't very close. Not since she was eight or so, about a year after I married him. That was the year she just seemed to become his child, more than mine.

He took over all the discipline when she was eight, and she did seem to need a lot of it, more than she ever had before. Well, I just didn't see what had happened, because she never said anything to me, and we weren't very close. It was always her and him.''

There were a number of things I wanted to say, but I kept my mouth firmly closed. The woman talked on.

''I should have believed her, I guess, when she was ten, but she was a difficult little girl.''

Funny thing.

''Anyway, a few years later, she was thirteen, I walked in on them. First I thought, maybe she seduced him? Men are so weak. But no, I remembered how she'd tried to tell. How she said it started when she was just eight. I threw him out of the house. Can you imagine? I actually thought about blaming her.''

I could imagine. I'd been a teacher for enough years. A case or two. No one I knew well. Always a girl in someone else's class. I wanted to ask where her bathroom was, go there and wash my face and my hands, pat cold water on my eyes. Eight years old.

''And that was four years ago that you found them together?''

''Yes. She's seventeen now. But really, it didn't seem to matter very much that I threw him out. Jane and I haven't gotten along too well since then, either. She's willful. Does what she wants to do, tells me—told me—to go to hell once or twice.''

"I'm sure she'll get over that." I was not at all sure Jane would get over any of it.

"My throwing him out, it didn't make Jane and me any closer. It just made us poorer. I managed to keep the property, but we had to move back here and rent out the big house to tenants. I had to take the job hostessing at DaVinci's restaurant. That was all right. But now she's disappeared." Mrs. Clapton was looking angry again. "It doesn't seem right, does it?"

"No, it sure doesn't. . . ."

"I don't think I should be punished for this for the rest of my life. I wish she'd just come back. I'm worn out. First the police, and they never really tried to find her anyway, and now this. I'm so tired. I wish she'd just come back."

I didn't go to the bathroom and I didn't get up and walk out. I stayed in that chair and kept on asking questions.

"We'll find her, Mrs. Clapton. The stepfather, has Jane seen him since he moved out?"

"Certainly not."

Still, he was someone I'd have to talk to. Once, anyway.

"Where does he live now?" Mrs. Clapton went to a secretary occupying a good portion of the room's south wall—a piece of furniture that, like everything else in the room, belonged in the bigger house at the front of the lot—and took a small address book out of a drawer.

"I don't know where he lives, but this is his office."

I pulled out my notebook and wrote down the

Oakland address and phone number she recited to me, glancing again at the long list of questions I wanted to ask.

"About Jane's job at the supermarket," I began. "Did she talk much about the people there? Did she have a lot of friends at work?"

She shrugged. "I know that Mark, that boy she was dating, he worked there. And she mentioned the manager, I forget his name, once or twice. She didn't talk about the job much."

"Surely she must have said something when one of her teachers was killed there."

"Oh, she told me about him being dead, and I asked her what people thought, but all she said was 'It was some maniac, that's what they think.' If you want to find out anything about what goes on at that market, Ms. Lake, you'll have to talk to the people there."

I nodded. "I'm planning to. But how did Jane feel about the murder? Did she see the body?"

"Well, she was upset, of course, but she didn't talk about it, just told me it happened and went to her room. Like she always did."

The woman was hopeless. "All right, Mrs. Clapton. Now I'd like to look at Jane's room, and after that I'd like to talk to you a little more." I wanted to get away from her for a few minutes, get off by myself. "Are you up to it?" If I sounded sarcastic, she didn't seem to notice. She said yes, she thought she was, and led me to a small room at the back of the house. It had big windows looking out on an old plum tree that nearly filled the tiny backyard. Mrs. Clapton pulled the drapes closed with two quick jerks of the cord.

"Why don't you just look around, look at anything you want. I'll be in the kitchen."

I watched her escape, glad to be rid of her for a while, then pulled the drapes open again and stood beside the bed, feeling like an intruder. Jane's life had been filled with intrusions. Invasions. How had she lived through her childhood? How did she live with adolescence now?

The small cubicle, weeks after the departure of its occupant, did not feel deserted. It still held the impression, multiple images, really, of the teenage girl who had lived in it. And "lived in it" seemed to be the right term. It was a warm nest, a burrow, a hideaway. It had been cleaned recently; I saw no dust on its surfaces. But its personality was intact, and it didn't match the rest of the house.

The furnishing was spare, and the colors were earth tones. No cool pastels. The spread on the single twin bed was brown, the throw pillows were red and orange, the rug was brown and white, the drapes deep red. There were a few books on a pine shelf, and on the white walls hung five carefully framed pieces of art: a print of Van Gogh's *Sunflowers*, a movie poster for *Casablanca*, a playbill from the Berkeley Repertory Theater's performance of Moliere's *Misanthrope*, what looked like a blown-up newspaper photograph of the 1984 U.S. women's Olympic volleyball team, and a photo of the old "Hollywood" sign in the hills above LA.

I went to the bookshelf. Her class yearbook was resting on top. On the shelves below were a couple of romance novels, a young adult book about a teenage actress with an alcohol problem, three Agatha Christie mysteries, *The Accidental Tourist*, a book called *Modern Plays*, Shakespeare's tragedies, a collection of short stories, the medieval costume book she'd brought to class—thumbing through it, I found a not-very-good pencil sketch of a woman in a wimple and a man in armor—and two paperback self-help books, one on *Making Relationships Work* and one on recovering from childhood sexual abuse.

The closet held a lot of reasonably fashionable adolescent clothing, as did the chest of drawers. Exactly how much clothing had Jane taken with her? One suitcase? Two? What kinds of clothes?

I hesitated before opening the top drawer of the small student desk. This was an even deeper invasion of privacy, but Jane was in trouble, and the whole point of this job was Jane's trouble, wasn't it? Not my squeamishness. The drawer contained pencils, pens, blank note paper, a jumble of paper clips, and nothing else.

The next drawer yielded a tape recorder, an empty three-ring binder, and some old class notebooks. The label on the tape in the recorder said, LOSE WEIGHT THROUGH HYPNOSIS! Jane had not been overweight, but it wasn't unusual for teenage girls to think they were.

The drawer below that one held an assortment of photocopied playscripts with the words MUMMER'S CLUB on the covers. Under those was a pile of scraps and sheets of paper that proved to be a collection of immature and cliché-ridden but sweetly idealistic poetry, all on the topics of acting and becoming an actor. Nothing that went anywhere near real, deep feelings. And not a love poem in the bunch. Didn't even abused adolescents dream of love?

In the bottom drawer I found bank statements for both a checking and a savings account, the last ones a month old, but neither a savings book nor a checkbook. Just before she'd disappeared, Jane had had a thousand dollars in her checking account and two thousand more in her savings account. Scattered among the bank statements were the only signs of sentimentality I had yet found: a birthday card from Mark wishing a happy seventeenth to his sweetheart, several birthday and Christmas cards from her natural father, and several, as well, from her mother. There was nothing from her stepfather.

Nowhere in the desk did I find an address book, although I did come up with an old, wrinkled scrap of paper with Lorene's name and phone number on it. There was also a phone number without a name. I pocketed them both.

The top of the desk held an assortment of school debris, a package of number ten envelopes, a book of stamps, and a glass paperweight with a snowman inside, the kind you turn upside down to watch the snow fall.

A small table under the bookshelf held a collection of wooden boxes of various designs and sizes. One of them was a jewelry box, with the usual

pendants, bracelets, and earrings. The rest of the
boxes were empty, existing, apparently, only for
themselves. Was that possible? I wondered. Boxes
were places to hide things in. Places for secrets.
But maybe Jane had had enough of secrets as a
child. Maybe she liked collecting wooden boxes, secret places, and never putting anything in them.

I found Roberta Clapton sitting in the kitchen,
drinking more coffee, and sat down across from
her. I asked her if Jane had had any problems
with alcohol or drugs, any problems at school. I
asked which of Jane's clothes were missing. I mentioned the playscripts and the volleyball team
photo, and managed to get bits of information
about places Jane liked to go, her friends, interests, hobbies, and dreams. Mrs. Clapton didn't
know much about Jane's friends, but she had met
and liked Mark.

Did Jane have a diary? She didn't know. An
address book? Yes, and Mr. Broz had asked about
it and she'd looked, but Jane must have taken it.

I came away from the interview with a lot to
digest, and an ache in my stomach to match the
one in my head. I now knew that the young
woman I was looking for had left home with one
suitcase and, Mrs. Clapton thought, mostly casual
clothing, including a swimsuit. I knew that she
had played volleyball in junior high school, loved
movies and plays, wanted to be an actor and, her
mother said, live in Los Angeles. That, according to her mother, she didn't drink too much or
take drugs. That she had a self-centered damned

fool of a mother, and had lived a childhood night-
mare.

The car door was hot to the touch. A rush of
saunalike air enveloped me when I opened it. I
slid into the driver's seat, folded up the cardboard
windshield-shade, and tossed it in back. I opened
all the openable glass, spit on both my hands, ran
my palms lightly around the blistering-hot black
steering wheel, spit on my right hand again,
grasped the gear knob gingerly, and started the
engine. Billie Holiday wailed from all four
speakers. Not what I wanted to hear. I pushed
preset button two for KSFO, classic rock and roll,
and Buddy Holly lived—"That'll Be The Day."

Once the car got moving, it cooled off quickly.
I didn't. Even though I told myself that driving
too fast was reckless and stupid and wasn't going
to do anybody any good, I made a pimpmobile
eat my dust on Cedar, and my headache went
away. After I passed a black Camaro on the San
Pablo straightaway, my stomach felt better. By the
time I reached University, I was feeling fine and
was ready to get on with the next step or two.

The car, however, was not quite so ready. The
gas gauge needle was well below empty.

7

I turned onto University, heading toward the section where a row of cheap stucco motels gives the avenue that special, freeway-exit ambiance, looking for the gas station I remembered seeing on a corner there.

The self-serve island had a line of cars waiting; I decided to treat myself to the illusion that I had better things to do with my time than save money. I pulled into full-serve behind a woman in a pickup. The truck bore the bumper sticker MY OTHER CAR IS A BROOM. The attendant finished with the pickup, turned toward me, and smiled that leering smile I'd grown to loathe. "Can I help you, Ms. Lake?"

It was Pissed-off Purvis, wearing blue coveralls with his name, Gerald, embroidered above the pocket, and a cap pulled down to his eyebrows.

"I didn't know you worked here, Gerald," I said, probably implying, by my tone of voice, that if I had known I'd have gone somewhere else.

"About a year now. Want me to fill it up?" he purred.

I ignored what was probably meant as a double

entendre. "Fine. Go ahead. Super." I handed him the key to the gas cap, waited while he cleaned the windshield, and took him up on his offer to check the fluid levels.

When I paid him, I asked politely how he liked the job.

"It's great, Ms. Lake," he said. "A great spot for watching what you might call the passing parade." He smirked, jerking a thumb toward the motel across the street, and dropped my change into my palm. "Thank you very much. And you come back soon, okay?"

He watched while I steered the car around to the station's phone booth, but by the time I'd begun dialing he was busy with another customer.

"Clapton Realty," the soft male voice said. I asked to speak to Neil Clapton.

"Speaking."

I told him who I was and what I was doing—and that as Jane's stepfather, he was one of the people I wanted to talk to.

"Of course. Let me see how we can do this . . . Do you have time now?"

As a matter of fact I did. I had planned on stopping at home for a while before going on to Lorene's, but it was just past five o'clock and I wasn't due there for a couple of hours.

"Sure. I could meet you at your office."

"Fine, but there's just one problem. I'm expecting a call from a client. If he calls before we've finished talking I'll have to leave right away—kind of a problem situation, you understand. Want to give it a try?"

The office address was in Albany, just north of Berkeley. I told him I could be there in ten minutes.

I got there in eight, and found a note on the door: ''Sorry, my client called. I'll be in and out tomorrow, but I'll have some time. N.C.''

Reflecting crankily that an awful lot of my first day seemed to be dedicated to planning the second, I decided to take a dinner break.

8

The South Berkeley street where Lorene lived was not the kind of place I'd ever deliberately visit at night.

I drove south on Martin Luther King, Jr., Way. The street, a major north-south route through Berkeley and Oakland, used to be called Grove, but it had been renamed in the late Seventies in a well-meaning political gesture that had created havoc among truckers for a few years until some clever bureaucrat had suggested adding signs that said "Old Grove Street" at a couple of main intersections. Most people didn't know what the hell to call it, since there was already a King street in Berkeley and the whole name was a mouthful. It was rapidly becoming MLK.

I turned right at a corner liquor store that had its security gate—the kind that covers the entire front of a business—rolled back just enough to let the customers in the door. A group of half a dozen young black men stood on the corner, talking and watching passing cars. A couple of men were talking with the driver of a parked car. I didn't know for sure, of course, that anyone on the corner that night was dealing or buying crack, that any of them were gang members, or that any of them were armed, but it would have been a pretty good guess. There had been a gang shooting recently on this corner, a major bust a few months back, a dead body found in the backyard of a nearby restaurant, and a drive-by killing or two.

I found the house three-quarters of a block down, a small, gray, frame cottage with bars on the windows, squatting close beside a much bigger structure, a Fifties-built pink stucco apartment building with cardboard taped behind the broken glass of two upstairs windows. Three men, one middle-aged and two younger, were standing in front of the apartment building. The older guy was wearing an Oakland A's cap. He and one of the younger men glanced at me briefly. The third, who was either talking to his friends softly or muttering to himself, couldn't seem to decide which leg should hold most of his weight, and danced from one to the other as he stared at me, watching me park and get out of the car.

"Hey! Hey!" His suddenly loud, agitated calls followed me up the walk to the small gray house. The shrubs in the yard looked trimmed and tended. A tidy bed of petunias had been cut into the middle of the small mowed lawn. The porch light was on.

"Hey! Girl! Lookin' good!"

I knocked on the door. Lorene yanked it open so suddenly I felt as though it had been ripped away from my knuckles, glanced out at the three men on the sidewalk, sighed and said, "Hi, Ms. Lake. Come on in."

I followed her into a living room furnished with small, pretty pieces—lamps, tables, and a rocking chair, all of which looked as though they'd come from a relative who was young in the 1920s—that were completely dominated by a big lump of a beige sectional couch that had been cleaned many times and was worn to the threads on arms and back.

"Please sit down, Ms. Lake. My grandmother said to tell you she's sorry she can't come down from her bedroom this evening. She said she'd like to meet you." I mumbled some equally formal words of regret and sat on the sectional.

Lorene offered me a soda and I declined. Formalities over, she got right down to it.

"Now what's this all about?"

"I'm trying to find Jane."

"You some kind of policewoman? Is it like, you know, like that show *Jump Street,* where those dudes work undercover in school?"

"No. I'm really a teacher. This is just something . . . extra I'm doing, working with Broz."

Lorene shook her head. "Don't you make enough money teaching?"

Knowing Lorene, I had expected something of an inquisition, but I wasn't sure how to answer her. "Yes I do. Well, not exactly, but I'm not doing it for the money. I just want to do it."

"Why?" Lorene was clearly suspicious of my motives.

"That's personal. Lorene, there's no reason for you to distrust me. I just want to help Jane. And you're one of her best friends. You must know something about what's happened to her."

"You want to help Jane so much you're willing to be a cop to do it—like, part-time? Kind of risky."

I shrugged. "Maybe I want to take a risk."

Lorene's eyes grew even narrower. "Well, whatever. What do you think I can tell you about?"

I wondered about Lorene's behavior. She had always seemed to be a friendly, open, intelligent kid. Her guarded attitude could mean she was hiding something important about Jane. On the other hand, it was possible I had simply offended her adolescent conservatism by not staying neatly in place as a teacher.

"I want to find Jane. I want to talk to her. I want to see if I can help her out of whatever trouble she's in."

Lorene appraised me shrewdly. "I bet you guys are really trying to find out who killed Mr. Anderson."

I smiled at her. "That would be good, too."

"Well, it wasn't Jane. Not a chance. She's too nice. Too damned nice. I know she couldn't have done it."

"I never thought she did. Why did she run off, Lorene?"

"You know, I'm thinking about becoming a lawyer. They investigate things, too."

"A lot of the time, I believe, they hire private investigators to do that work for them."

"Maybe I can hire you some time. You got any African-American blood?"

"Not that I know of."

"Too bad. You've really got a lot of nerve."

"Thank you. I think. But you're avoiding my questions. When did you last see Jane?"

"The day before she went. But I can't really help you, you know. I just don't know anything to help you with."

"You probably know more than you think you do. For instance, you must know how she feels about Mark. You must know what's been going on with them."

Lorene shrugged. "Not much. I mean, I think they still care about each other, and they were still dating and everything, but you know how that stuff goes."

"Have they been fighting? Was she seeing someone else—did she go somewhere to be with someone else?"

"No. She didn't have anybody else, I can tell you that." Lorene looked me straight in the eyes, an action which may or may not have had any significance.

"When you saw her, before she left, did she say she was going? Did she say *where* she was going?"

Lorene's eyes shifted away. "No."

"Was there any place you know of where she might have wanted to go? A place she talked about sometimes, a place she liked?"

"She talked about LA a lot, you know, because of the acting." I thought of Tito, looking for Jane in LA. Somehow I had the feeling that if Lorene was willing to mention it as a possibility, he wouldn't find her there.

"Is that where you think she went?"

"I don't know where she went."

"Broz called you and said he wanted to set up a talk with you about Jane. What did you think when you heard from him?"

"Nothing. Well, I mean, I didn't believe it. This is all so, well, so TV, you know? You sure you want to go into this line of work?"

"No."

"You carrying a gun?"

"No."

Lorene's eyebrows went up. "I think you better get one."

"Could we get back to Jane?"

Lorene shrugged, nodded. "Sure. But I don't know what to tell you."

"Did you call Mr. Broz and tell him Jane was in LA?"

"Someone did that? Well, it wasn't me."

I was not convinced. "Do you think she's just gone off somewhere, that she's okay?"

"You mean do I think she's dead or something? No. I don't think that."

"Do you think she could be in some kind of danger?"

"Well, shit—excuse me—everybody's in *some* kind of danger. What if she is? You think you can save her?"

"I'd like to think so."

Lorene's flash of belligerence subsided. "Well,

I'm sorry. I don't mean to sound like that, but you know, that girl could have used some saving a few years ago. You hear about that?"

"Yes. And you're right. But that was then, and this is now."

"Maybe she's got problems she needs to work out on her own."

"What if she can't?"

Lorene shook her head "I can't tell you what I can't tell you."

"But you two were friends. What did you talk about?"

"The future. Acting. Being a lawyer. Her getting away from her mother and me getting away from here. Mark. She really liked Mark. My boyfriends. She didn't talk all that much about her own personal life, just sometimes, like she was saving it up and then it would all come out at once."

"Lorene, I think you know the answers to some of my questions. I don't know why you won't talk to me. Are you protecting Jane, or someone else?"

"Even if I did know something, which I don't, maybe you and your boss don't know what you're doing, and you could hurt her, too. But I don't know anything about her going away or about Anderson. Sorry."

For the moment, I was stymied. I stood up.

"Okay, Lorene. Thank you for what you have felt able to tell me." I stuck out my hand and Lorene shook it.

"If I could help you more, you know, I would. But I can't."

"We'll talk again."

Lorene said nothing until we were both standing at the front door.

"Sometimes there's nothing you can do," she said. "Things just are the way they are." She opened the door. I stepped out. The three men were still standing on the sidewalk next door, talking. The hyperactive one glanced over at me.

"And if something's wrong, you just let it be that way? You live with it?"

"You stay away from it. Or if you can't stay away from it, you *get* away from it. Good night, Ms. Lake." She closed the door behind me.

One of the men moved down the walk, closer to my car—not the hyper one, the other young one, the silent one. By the time I'd reached the RX7, he was sitting on its sloping hood. The other two had moved closer.

"You'll have to get off my car. I'm leaving."

"She don't like you to sit on her car, Nathan." The hyper one giggled.

"This is my neighborhood." Nathan stared at her. "I sit where I want."

"I'm sure that's true. But my car and I are going now. You'll have to find something else to sit on."

"I'm sittin' here."

"Nathan . . ." The middle-aged man seemed to be thinking of intervening.

"Make her stay, Nathan, okay?"

"Shut up, Willie," the middle-aged man spoke again.

Nathan continued to stare at me. "This is *my* neighborhood," he said again.

"Fine. It's your neighborhood. But it's my car."

I was scared of Nathan. He had dead mean eyes. I got in the car, locked the doors, and started the engine. Despite the fact that his butt was planted on my right headlight, I turned the switch to raise the lights. The mechanism goosed him and he slid partway off the hood. I threw the gear stick into first and gunned it away from the curb. Nathan fell off.

I looked out my rearview mirror. Nathan and Willie were standing in the street. The older man was gone. As I approached the next intersection west, I noticed that the right headlight had never made it all the way up and would probably need repair. The next thing I noticed was the big old American car—a beat-up, dented and scratched monster from the early Seventies—rounding the corner, swerving to a stop in front of me, blocking the narrow street. I slammed on my brakes, paralyzed for a moment with indecision. Where could I go?

The driver jumped out of the car. He was wearing an oversized, long raincoat and a pair of pantyhose stretched over his face. I heard myself scream, and then I heard the scream fade to a growl deep in my throat as he ran toward me.

Enough! What am I doing, I asked myself, waiting to see whether this grotesque creature has an AK-47 under that coat? I yanked the lever into reverse, shifted around in my seat—Nathan and Willie were still standing in the street, and their older friend had rejoined them—and stepped on the gas.

I have never been that great at backing up. My progress down the street at thirty? forty?—I wasn't watching my speedometer—miles an hour in reverse, was erratic. I scraped the fender of a parked car and came within inches of hitting Nathan, Willie, and their ineffectual pal. I had nearly reached MLK before I dared glance back down the way I had come. The big car was gone. So were Lorene's friendly neighbors.

I couldn't stop to leave a note with my phone number on the windshield of the car I'd hit. I would just have to pretend it belonged to Nathan. Still in reverse, I shot back onto MLK, earning the amusement of the liquor store recreational group and a horn-blast from a passing—swerving—car, and headed north.

Tito and Lorene were right. I needed a gun.

9

Nine o'clock. I was due at the client's in half an hour. If I wanted to get there on time I'd have to start out now, to allow for getting lost once, briefly, on the dark and winding hill roads.

At the same time, I was not ready to drive those roads—not with the adrenaline scouring my innards, not while I was shaking with fear and excitement. And the client didn't need to see me this way. I stopped at a diner on Telegraph and, after checking my car and finding a badly scraped fender and a headlight truly stuck at half-mast, went inside, ordered a cup of coffee and a doughnut, and used the pay phone to call and say I had been detained by the investigation and would be about twenty minutes late. The woman who took the message, his wife I suppose, said she would tell him when he got home.

Naturally I had to rerun the scene once in my mind as a total victory: I have a gun, I pull it, I capture the masked strangler and take him in. But generally speaking, I was pretty pleased with myself, aside from a touch of guilt about the car I'd scratched. My escape had been skillful and daring, if not elegant. The problem was, the freakish sight of my attacker had crippled my perceptions. I wanted to be able to say he was tall or short or black or white or dark-haired or blond. That he had a limp. That he was a one-armed man. I was pretty sure I'd seen two arms, and that he had not limped. As for the rest of it, he had looked enormous in the big coat and he had been slightly bent over, I thought, as he ran toward me. He could have been any height over five-seven. He could even have been a woman.

I would have to learn to be more observant under pressure, to snap mental pictures while running for my life.

And then there was the second major question: Did he have anything to do with the case, or was he just another bizarre manifestation, like Nathan and Willie, of life in the East Bay? If he was connected with the case, was he following me or watching Lorene? If he was following me, he was one of the people who knew I was working on the case—and knew where to find me.

And if he was following me, why was I driving a red car?

The coffee and doughnut didn't do much for my heart rate, but the time spent with them calmed the tremors. I set out for the Berkeley Hills.

The street where the client lived showed up on the map as a tiny parenthesis stuck on the end of a small street that ran into another small street that ran into a longer street that eventually bisected a main road. The kind of woodsy retreat where the residents all have carports cut into the sides of hills or built out over the abyss, and visitors have to park halfway up a clay bank because the road itself is ten feet wide.

Wahlman had one of the overhanging carports, and there was only one car parked in it. I hesitated. I could pull in there, taking a chance on irritating a yet-to-arrive family member and violating the protocol of the hills, or I could park against a bank of blackberry on one side of the road or the patch of poison oak on the other. I didn't do any of those things. I drove another hundred feet and found a slightly more hospitable spot, a dirt shoulder of sun-baked, rutted clay.

The client had been the last person on my mind that day, so I turned on my dome light, pulled out my notebook, and did a quick review. His name was Andrew Wahlman. He had not lived with Jane and her mother since the girl was four years old, thirteen years ago. He had supported them both, he said, until the mother remarried, and then had continued to contribute to Jane's support. He had remarried soon after the mother had and started another family, and had not seen much of Jane since then. Wahlman was in some kind of investment business, and had apparently invested in the right things at the right times because he had money or lived like he did. The police, he believed, were doing little or nothing to find his missing daughter, and a friend had recommended Tito for the job. That was pretty much the story on him.

It was hard to believe that, as recently as yesterday, I had been nervous about talking to him, worried that my lack of experience would show. I felt that I was beginning to get the hang of this detective stuff, and while I had not yet achieved the level of a Spade, a Marlowe, a Warshawski, or a McCone, I thought I was already a cut or two above Nancy Drew.

I trekked back to the Wahlman gate, then down a steeply sloping walk to the door.

All I could see of the house was that it looked big and well-kept. The shrubs and trees and the landscape itself made any other appraisal difficult.

A large, well-dressed man answered the door.

"Barrett Lake?"

I nodded. "Andrew Wahlman?"

"Come in, please."

He guided me through the foyer politely, but without friendliness, businesslike and dressed in a business suit that looked expensive and tailored. The living room was three steps down from the entry and was, at least by my standards, immense. A wall of glass looked out on a view of the flatlands, the bay, the Bay Bridge, and San Francisco beyond. To the right, I could just barely make out a piece of the Golden Gate. The fog was a thin gray-white net of tatters and shreds, pierced by the lights of San Francisco and reaching out for Berkeley.

A shade too briskly, Wahlman asked me to "please sit down."

I sat, on one of a pair of white couches that seemed to be made of pillows and were set at right angles to the glass wall. Wahlman remained standing, his physical presence large and maybe just a touch daunting in its well-pressed perfection. I heard voices in another room, a woman and a child, I thought, and the drone of a TV monologue.

"Can I get you something to drink? Coffee? Beer? Wine?"

"I'd love a glass of white wine."

He nodded once, and strode to a wet bar at the far end of the room, which gave me time to look around more carefully. Glass tables, a large, pale, flowered Chinese rug. On the wall opposite the windows was a white brick fireplace, set in a conversation pit. A fire pit, I thought. We keep returning to the caves. A large—four-by-five?—oil painting done in slashes and blocks of muted color hung over the fireplace, fulfilling its decorator-selected function of not competing with the expensive rug.

There were no books anywhere in sight in the room, and no other art.

Wahlman returned with the wine. He had not gotten anything to drink for himself.

Still standing over me, he said, "Why is it that women always drink white wine?"

I leaned back to look up at him, trying to avoid craning my neck. His eyes were hard, his mouth quirked at one end. This man spent too much time doing deals, playing King of the Mountain. He was holding on to the high ground, making me struggle to climb alongside. I would not struggle, but I wouldn't let him keep the high ground, either. I stood up and walked past him to the window, smiling into my wineglass.

"I don't know why women do anything. I like white wine."

I turned and faced him. If he wanted to stand through this whole interview, I would stand, too. I hadn't been a school system employee for all those years without learning to play stupid games. I smiled at him again.

"Would you like to ask me questions," I said, "or should I just tell you what I can after one day on the case?"

Wahlman didn't want to stand anymore. He waved me back to the couch and sat down on its twin, facing me across an expanse of glass table top crowned with a bowl of slightly wilted red roses. Now that he wasn't crowding me and trying to overwhelm me, I was able to notice that he was a fairly attractive man. Mid-forties, graying dark brown hair, no more than an extra ten pounds around the middle. He crossed his legs. Not so much as a quarter inch of skin showed above his sock. He cleared his throat and recrossed his legs. I caught myself looking at the clean line of his calf and raised my eyes to his face again. He seemed to be waiting for me to say something more. I decided to outwait him, cocking my head politely, attentively.

Finally he spoke.

"I just wanted to get a look at you. Talk to you. Broz says you're competent and experienced, but I hired him to find my daughter, not you. I wanted to assure myself that you weren't just some bimbo he kept around for fun.''

The man couldn't stop testing. I squelched a rush of anger and tried to think of him as a veneered Pissed-off Purvis. That made me laugh.

Which made him frown. He had not expected me to laugh. Smiling at him in a friendly fashion, I said, ''I hope I can set your mind at ease, Mr. Wahlman.'' He almost smiled back. At least his body relaxed slightly.

''Okay, Ms. Lake. What are your thoughts about my daughter's disappearance?''

I sipped my wine. ''It looks like she left on her own, and I'm following up on some leads. But I don't know enough about the case yet to have any coherent thoughts about where she might be.'' He raised his eyebrows. Why? Probably because I was being too honest. He was not a man to be too honest with. I decided to put it back on him. ''I'm learning about Jane, about her habits and her friends. Maybe there's something you can add that you didn't tell Tito when you hired us?''

''Whatever I told him is what I know. That's all I have. I'm afraid I don't know my daughter very well.'' He sighed, his defenses down for a moment, his face relaxed and sagging into lines of worry. ''And that's my fault. But I thought she'd be okay.'' Suddenly he glanced at me suspiciously, as if I were going to spring at his throat. I gave him my best impression of a benign look. He turned his face away, gazing toward the window wall at either his panoramic view of the magic kingdom or his own reflection.

"You know," I said, "that a teacher of Jane's was murdered a couple of weeks before she disappeared. That may or may not—"

He swung back toward me and cut off my words. "Yes. I've heard something to that effect. But I'm paying you people to find my daughter, not to run off on a wild, glamorous goose chase, looking for some irrelevant killer. And I'm paying plenty."

But not Tito's highest price, I thought. And the thought must have showed in my face because he looked down at the frayed roses and said, "Plenty. And it's not like money's all that easy to come by these days. . . ."

When he faced me again the cold, appraising look was still there, but it didn't look as seamless as it had before. The man was worried and he was tired.

"Tell me how you're going to find her."

"I've started with her home and with some of the people who do know her well, and I'm following her trail." I finished my wine.

"That's it? You're following her trail? Like a bloodhound? Give me some specifics."

I didn't have too many of those to give him.

"Well, of course, we've already made sure that the Berkeley police put her on the National Crime Information Computer. That's the FBI system, you know, and all the local departments can call up information from it on their own computers. The NCIC is broken down into categories—wanted, runaways, that kind of thing. The police can't do much more than that, and it's not much—because there are several million names on it and no one checks it unless the missing person is actually picked up." Or found dead, but I didn't say that. He nodded, looking thoughtful.

"She's registered with the state clearinghouse and with the National Center for Missing and Exploited Children."

"I know that. Mr. Broz asked me to leave a message on their hotline for her. I did. What else?"

"We've got feelers out at all the local runaway shelters." Tito had taken care of that right away, too. And none of what he'd done had turned up word of Jane. "I've visited her mother, taken a look at Jane's room, gone through her things. I've found some clues to her life there, leads to follow. I've talked to a friend of hers. I'll check out all her friends, her teachers"—he did not have to know I was one of them—"all the places she spent time, find out if there was a problem at school, at home, a place she's been dreaming about running off to. What we do after that depends on what we find."

"And what else?" he wanted to know.

I sighed, as though I still wanted to please but was beginning to weary. I wasn't, but the truth was, I had nothing else to say.

"If this is a test, Mr. Wahlman, I think my time would be better spent working on the case. And I have some questions I want to ask you."

"You must have been doing something pretty important tonight—it made you late for this appointment."

I'd been hoping he'd ask that.

"Actually," I said, "I was busy escaping from a masked attacker on a South Berkeley crack street."

"What the hell were you doing there?"

"Talking to Jane's best friend." He looked horrified. "She's a good kid," I said through my teeth, thinking, where does this guy come off . . . ? "She just lives there."

He held up his hands. "All right. All right. You understand why I've been questioning you this way, I hope? I'm just trying to feel that this is the right course. Checking out the lay of the land, so to speak. Surely you see nothing wrong with reassuring a client. I have to do that all the time."

I inclined my head. "Yes. I understand."

"Well then, ask your questions."

I took out my notebook, the brand-new one I'd picked out at the stationer's that morning, no longer new-looking; its cover bent, many of its pages scribbled with tight notes and too many question marks.

"I'm not clear on the timelines in your daughter's life. You and the mother separated when she was four. How long after that was it before she remarried?"

"Three years."

"And you remarried when?"

"Does this really matter?" He was giving me more respect now. The question held more curiosity than doubt.

"Yes." I didn't know whether it mattered or not, I just wanted the information.

"Jane was eight, so it was about a year after her mother got married again."

"And you were still seeing her often then?"

"Not often, no. She had a stepfather. I thought he was a pretty useless type, but he was her new family. I was starting a new family. Our marriage—mine to her mother—hadn't been very happy. I suppose I didn't want to interfere. I suppose I thought it would be better to let things change." He was looking down at his hands, folded between his knees. A "pretty useless type"? Mild words. Did he even know? "Don't get me wrong. I still kicked in for support, and I still saw her sometimes. Just not very often."

"Did Jane tell you what her stepfather was doing to her?"

He continued to look at his hands. "I didn't find out until after he was gone."

"Did it ever occur to you to prosecute him?" It hadn't occurred to Jane's mother.

"Her mother thought it would be best if we just let Jane try to forget it, that nobody needed to go through that. I thought she'd be okay."

But she wasn't okay now, if she ever had been, and he knew that, and it seemed that his guilt was forcing him to spend some of his money on detectives.

I stood. "I think that's all I need for now, Mr. Wahlman."

He got up quickly, walked around the glass table top, gripped my hand.

"And you'll keep me informed of your progress?"

"Of course. You'll get our reports regularly."

"I think we'll get along just fine." He let go of my hand and walked with me to the door. As I was leaving the house he said, "I don't imagine you got much information about Jane from her mother. I don't think she paid much attention to the kid, if you know what I mean."

I didn't answer him. I just said good night.

10

Tito called early the next morning. The LA trip had been phony. Jane was not with her cousin there, he said, and although the cousin had willingly supplied the names of a couple of family friends in the area, he'd found no sign of the missing girl.

He asked how I was doing.

"I'm doing great," I said, convinced, now, that this was so. "I don't know a lot yet, but—"

"Didn't expect you to. Listen, I'm running up to Santa Rosa on another case, but I should be back by three. Why don't you meet me in the office then, we'll go over what you've got, talk about your next moves. Okay?"

I couldn't imagine what he could have going in Santa Rosa that was more fascinating than what I was doing, but if I had to wait until three to talk to him, that was all right; I had other things to do. And I could use my free time very well to think about the case and the questions one day's work had raised, to collar some people and make some calls.

Rob Harwood was one of the first people on my

list. He'd practically broken out in a sweat when I'd tried to talk to him about Jane the day before. He needed pinning down.

I stopped at his classroom between first and second periods but he wasn't there. I went to see Olivia in the office.

"I need to catch Rob Harwood today," I said casually. "Is he around?"

She gave me an over-the-bifocals look and brushed back her long gray-brown hair.

"He's around."

"Maybe I can see him at lunch—does he still take it at noon?" I didn't have any idea when he took lunch, but noon was when I did.

She checked her lists. "Yes, indeed, Barrett. Noon it is. And I'll bet I know what you want to talk to him about."

I gazed back at her innocently.

"It's all over school this morning, your being a detective."

Well, that was hardly a surprise. Harwood knew. Lorene knew.

"And Rob must have known Jane Wahlman pretty well, her being in the Mummers. Isn't that right?"

"She was in the Mummers."

"And girls are always getting crushes on Rob."

"Oh? Is that so?" I didn't want to push Olivia. She's the kind who gossips whether she knows anything or not, always acts like she knows the unknowable, and shuts up just when she gets you interested—to cover up for her own lack of solid information.

"Everyone knows that!" she shook her head at me, pitying my ignorance. "But I've already said more than enough, I'm sure." She straightened her glasses and bent to her desk again.

I caught Rob in the hall just before third period. "We have to talk," I said. "What about lunch?"

"I'm really sorry, Barrett, but I'm busy today."

"Maybe tomorrow then. At noon?"

"Not possible. I go at one."

"Not according to Olivia." Olivia didn't make that kind of mistake.

He flushed pink. "You checked on me in the office? You've got a lot of gall, Barrett. I can't believe you'd do that. Olivia's such a gossip—what are you trying to do to me?"

I thought he was really overreacting.

"Rob, relax, will you? Now come on, how about lunch today?"

"I told you. I'm busy." He glared at me. "Why don't you ask who I'm having lunch with? Or maybe you want to invite yourself along?"

That's an idea, I thought.

"Don't be silly. What about tonight?"

"Look, today's just not the right day. But I said I'd talk to you"—he sighed and gritted his teeth— "and I will. How about sometime tomorrow?"

"Tomorrow's fine, but let's get specific. Tomorrow right after school?"

He shrugged. "Okay. Tomorrow at three-fifteen at The Elbow Room, down on Shattuck. Do you know the place?" I did.

Mark was even worse. I caught him on the run

and told him I wanted to talk to him—and I wanted to do it that day.

He nodded, his face expressionless.

"I'm like really busy, Ms. Lake. What's this all about, anyway?"

I told him about working with Tito. He nodded again.

"I heard about that. But I'm in kind of a hurry. And I've got to go to work later. Besides, I don't know anything that would help you."

"After work. I can come over to your house after work."

"Okay. Whatever. I'll get back to you later." And he was off at a gallop.

After the reception I had gotten from Rob and Mark, I was startled when Lorene approached me—and in a friendly fashion.

"I'm sorry about the stuff that happened to you last night," she said. "We got some fools living on that block. I'd have helped, but you took care of it pretty good on your own."

"You mean that guy in the pantyhose and raincoat does that kind of thing all the time?"

She stared at me. "I meant about Nathan and Willie and them. I heard Nathan and came to the window. But I don't know anything about pantyhose." She laughed. "Pantyhose?"

I told her about it and her expression grew serious.

"I did hear a couple of shouts and a little other noise, but I thought you were long gone by then, and, you know, it's not always a quiet street."

Now there's an understatement, I thought.

"So you've never seen anyone like that before?"

"I think I'd remember him! I hope you'll excuse me for saying it, Ms. Lake, but like I said, you've got a lot of nerve being a detective." She shook her head and began to walk away. I stopped her.

"Lorene, what kind of relationship did Jane have with Rob Harwood?"

"Rob Harwood?" She studied my face, but I couldn't tell what she found there. "She thought a lot of him. He taught her a lot." She hesitated, then, looking somewhere over my shoulder: "She flirted with him, too, I think." Without looking directly at me again, she added, "I got to go. See you." And she went.

Ten minutes before my usual lunch period I was sitting in my car in the parking lot, waiting for Rob Harwood to come out of the building. I had decided to take him up—after a fashion—on his invitation to lunch. I wanted to see what it was he was so damned busy doing.

He came out just after noon. When he was half a block up the street, I pulled into traffic behind his white Subaru four-wheel drive. I knew he lived in Oakland, not off a dirt road somewhere in Sonoma, but decided, charitably, that he probably drove to Tahoe a lot in the winter.

He took Telegraph to Ashby, where he turned left. I nearly lost him before I was able to make the turn, too, catching a glimpse of his car several blocks ahead signaling a right at College.

I passed a van by sliding around its right side at Regent and turned at the block before College to avoid the main intersection's traffic mess. When I reached College I checked the street to my left to make sure he hadn't parked, then made my turn. He was less than a block ahead of me.

We passed Alcatraz and crossed into Oakland. One block farther south, he parked and went into a trendy diner where I'd had breakfast a few times. I wondered whether my car or my person would be more conspicuous. I decided that I was smaller and not quite as bright. I walked slowly, on the other side of the street, toward the diner.

The tall, pretty woman coming down Claremont Avenue looked familiar. She reached the door of the diner just as Rob opened it from the inside, waving her in, smiling.

I knew her because I'd seen her at a few faculty events. She was Mrs. William Anderson. I don't know what I had expected to see, but she wasn't it.

I waited until they came out again, half an hour later, and got into separate cars. They both drove North along College, but when he turned at Ashby, she kept going. I stuck with him all the way back to school.

That afternoon I managed to reach Neil Clapton and make a firm appointment. I also filled in my notes, wrote down some questions for the people I was going to see, and speculated for a long time on the relationship between Rob Harwood and Elizabeth Anderson.

Tito found it fascinating, too.

He was waiting at the office when I got there. He looked a little tired.

"Too bad LA was a bust," I said.

He shrugged. "Part of the game. I do have one little piece of information for you, though. Well, negative information, I guess you could call it. I got a pal with a computer who hacks into the Social Security records. I checked in with him last week. He left a message on the office phone machine while I was gone—she's either not working or she's not using her number."

"Where'd you get her Social Security number, from her mother?"

"Sure. It's all over Jane's bank statements." Of course. The ones I'd seen.

"And if she'd been working under her number, we would have known where she was working. . . ."

"Right. Case closed. A lot of times it's that easy. But no such luck on this one. Now, what have you been doing?"

I told him, dwelling on Rob and the widow Anderson, segueing into the masked attacker, and finishing up with my plans for that afternoon and evening.

We talked about the people connected with Jane, besides Harwood, the ones I'd had some contact with: her boyfriend, her best friend, her boss, her mother, her stepfather, and her father.

"Lorene knows something," I said. "And I think Mark does, too."

Tito shrugged. "Could be."

"I know I'm supposed to be looking for Jane, but what if Anderson's murder is the most important link to her disappearance, and what if his killer is the only route to finding her? Or finding out what happened to her?"

"You're letting yourself think in circles, Barrett. You a baseball fan?"

"Yes. Well, I'm an A's fan. And the Twins."

"Let's stick with the A's for a minute. You know what Carney Lansford tells his team?"

I love Carney Lansford. "Stay focused."

"Yeah. And it works pretty well for them. Your job is to find Jane. You focus on that and everything else will clear itself up."

Then he delivered a brief, probably accurate, and slightly irritating performance evaluation.

"About the way you've got things all planned out for today—you're kind of an overachiever, aren't you? I mean, you're scheduling yourself too tight. You're not leaving yourself any flexibility. And you're giving all these people too much warning. Try to come at them more when they aren't expecting you, like following Harwood. That was good. Other than that, you're handling it. I'm going to leave the case in your capable hands.

"But first, if we can squeeze it into your busy schedule, we're going to go and pick out a gun for you."

11

The gun shop was enormous and had existed, probably on that same Oakland corner, since 1945.

All along the right wall, as we entered, were hunting rifles. Dozens of them, beautiful and ugly in their wood-and-steel simplicity. The long counter was a glass case in which lay handguns of amazing variety. To the left and up ahead of us, bows and arrows—longbow and crossbow—fishing tackle, backpacking gear. A large sign listed the store's gunsmithing capabilities, from cleaning and oiling to custom design.

And up high on the walls, above the rifles, above the sign, were the heads of slaughtered animals. A moose. Several bucks. A boar. If Gilda were to see this place, I thought, she'd take an axe to it like Carrie Nation. I dropped my eyes, not really wanting to see, and they lighted on a ledge, below the heads and above the guns, on which were artfully arranged small scenarios of stuffed animals—here a squirrel and a rabbit sharing a log, there a trio of dead ducks.

The ducks brought a flashback to a childhood scene at my parents' store, and for just a moment

I felt all the horror and pride I had felt during that incident nearly thirty years ago.

Some of our neighbors and customers had migrated from the small towns of Minnesota and the Dakotas, farm towns. They hunted and fished as a matter of course. But one day—I was about twelve years old, I think, it was a Saturday, and I was working with my father while my mother spent the afternoon at her card club—one of those customers made too big a point of his hobby.

His name was Einar Peterson. He was a nice enough guy and a very good customer with a credit account. He strode into the store, smiling, cheery, carrying a large canvas sack that looked dark around the bottom.

"Hey, Ralph," he said to my father. "I got a present for you and your family." He reached in the sack and pulled out three bloody duck corpses.

I had seen dead fowl before, in the kosher butcher shop, but I loved animals and the sight had disturbed me. My father had spoken affectionately, many times, of the families of ducks he used to feed on the pond near his village in Russia. Yet we ate chickens. We had even eaten duck. The whole subject was puzzling to me.

Einar tried to pass the birds to my father, who kept his hands firmly at his sides.

"You shot them yourself?" he asked softly. His face was even paler than usual.

"Sure did," said Einar, perhaps not the most perceptive man in the world.

"You murdering bastard!" my father yelled.

''Put those poor things back in the bag and you, you get the hell out of my store!''

Einar forgave him within a week. After all, everyone knew my father read too much, frowned too much, and was probably a little crazy. Yet despite my own confusion—and perhaps his own—I knew he had done something wonderful.

And now here I was, standing in a gun store, thinking of Gilda and of my father, feeling like a spy for the Doris Day Animal League.

But I'm not buying a handgun so I can shoot the innocent, I told myself. I'm buying a handgun to defend myself against the guilty. Guilty without trial? Hell, yes. If a man comes at you on a dark street with a weapon or a threat, he's guilty.

Tito and I were looking down into the glass case. I didn't know what I was looking at, but I assumed Tito did.

''Can I help you?''

The man on the other side of the case was slight and gray and looked like a Presbyterian minister.

''We need to buy a gun for the lady,'' Tito told him.

''I'm not really a lady,'' I said. The man did not smile. ''But I don't know anything about guns. What would you recommend?''

He nodded and looked thoughtful. ''Well, for a woman, definitely not an automatic. Revolvers are simpler to operate under stress.''

''Simpler?'' I repeated. I smiled. ''You make us sound like idiots.''

He looked at me, and apparently decided I was okay despite my sharp edges. He laughed.

"No, that's not what I mean. I mean a woman who doesn't know guns. Some women who've been in law enforcement and have a lot of training with weapons use automatics. But they're much harder to use." He pulled a black-and-silver square-looking job out of a case at our left that held maybe three dozen square-looking jobs of various sizes and designs. "This is a nine-millimeter semiautomatic. See, you have to pull this slide back before you can pull the trigger." He yanked the entire top of the pistol back and then forward again.

I held out my hand and he gave me the gun. I pulled at the slide, tentatively. Nothing. I was, I thought, a reasonably strong person. I gritted my teeth and yanked the thing hard. It slid.

"That's too much work," I agreed. "Why would anyone, even a very strong person, want to bother?"

He shrugged. "Automatics hold more bullets."

I thought the basic six-shooter would be good enough for me. All of us, Tito and I on one side of the case and the expert—his name was Edwards, Jonathan Edwards, he told us—on the other side, moved down a few feet to the revolvers.

They look more like guns anyway, I thought, with wooden grips and round barrels. And somehow less nasty, although I didn't know why that was so.

"Now what exactly are you going to be using this gun for?" he asked.

"She's training to be a private investigator," Tito said. "She'll be carrying it."

"Okay. Well, you don't want anything too small, but you don't want to be carrying anything too clumsy, either." He pulled two pistols out of the case. They were both on sale.

The smaller of the two was a pretty little thing with a two-inch barrel. A Smith & Wesson .38 special, Edwards said, with a five-shot cylinder, a blue finish, a smooth combat trigger, and a round butt. The stock was checkered walnut. I picked it up. Very light. Thirteen and a half ounces, he said. Light and small, a palm-of-the-hand gun.

"Why is it called 'special'?" I asked.

"Part of the caliber description, ma'am. It's a thirty-eight, but the special is a longer and more powerful cartridge."

The second one was bigger and heavier, a six-shot .357 magnum with a two-and-a-half-inch barrel, stainless steel. It weighed thirty and a half ounces. It also had a walnut stock and the popular round butt. It cost fifty dollars more than the smaller one. Edwards said a heavier gun was more accurate, that it wouldn't jump as much in my hand.

I was attracted to the .38 because it would be easy to carry and easy to conceal. I liked the idea of the .357 magnum because I wanted to shoot accurately, if I was going to shoot at all. What I finally decided on was a heavier, slightly longer .38 special—nineteen ounces with a two-and-a-half-inch barrel.

We talked a while about single-action and

double-action—the pistol I was buying was double, but could be single if you wanted to go through the extra step and pull the hammer back, which, he explained, allowed you to exert less pressure on the trigger and, therefore, aim better.

I wrote a check for four hundred and fifty dollars and Edwards said there was a fifteen-day waiting period. He also said that if I was going to carry the gun concealed on my person or in my car I would need a permit, which I could get from the Alameda County Sheriff's Department.

I could see that this was all going to take longer than I'd hoped.

And what *about* carrying the gun? I did plan to, and at that point it occurred to me to ask him how—or where.

"Oh, yes," he said. "Well, I've got a catalogue here somewhere. . . ." He groped around behind the counter. "There are specially-made handbags that policewomen use. . . ."

He pulled out the catalogue, thumbed through it, and showed me the page with the bags. Fine leather, it said, in black, brown, and tan. There were two basic models: one that came with a kind of flat rack or insert that held a holster, ammunition, and handcuffs, and one with a simpler zipper pocket on the outside. I wrote down the particulars.

Edwards said it would take a couple of weeks to get one, so I should call him as soon as I decided which one I wanted. I thought I might want two, one brown and one black.

When we turned to go, Edwards said, "Ms.

Lake? You come back any time you want to buy an automatic.''

I told him I would.

''You got time to run out to Hayward to apply for your permit?'' Tito asked as we got back into my car.

I thought I did, so we headed for the freeway and the Sheriff's Department Identification Bureau. I filled out the form, posted an insurance bond, and was told that a detective would review my application, that if all went well, I'd have the permit in a couple of weeks, and that I would be required to attend a range program twice a year.

All of which seemed perfectly reasonable. Twenty minutes later I dropped Tito off at the office and made my way through rush-hour traffic to the northern end of Berkeley and the SaveMor Market.

12

The store was medium-large for a supermarket, not as gigantic as the average Safeway. The layout was fairly standard, with the meat department at the far left and produce at the far right.

Supermarkets, I reflected for perhaps the hundredth time, just don't smell the way a grocery store should. Some of them, the ones with lobster tanks, often smell very bad, but most of them don't smell at all.

They don't have the right noises, either, and nothing feels the way it should.

The store I grew up in smelled wonderful: the musty cherry and banana ice of popsicles; the black, earthy licorice; the sugary vanilla of the bulk cookies in their bins; the dusty, unwashed russet potatoes in their bushel baskets; the bologna, salami, and summer sausage in the meat case; the ripe melons and peaches in the front window; even the dregs of soda—we called it "pop"—and stale three-two beer in the empties stacked in cases in the back room, and my father's unfiltered Camels.

The sounds and textures aren't as vivid in

memory, but reliving the smells recalls them. The slam of the screen door, the ring of the cash register, the shout of ''Kike!'' from a neighborhood kid racing past the entrance, the smooth, uneven feel of the gray, sawdust-swept wooden floor on the soles of my bare feet.

People used to hang out, too, sitting on the long board on the front radiator, talking for a while. We all knew each other. We knew who was beating his wife and kids, who had been laid off, who spent the grocery money on beer, whose kids had run away or gone to juvey.

If a man had been murdered in our store, we would have noticed right away.

I located the cereal aisle, where Anderson had died. Cereal was one over from housewares, which was next to the produce department. At right angles to the cereal, at the far end, was butter and margarine. At the entry end was an express checkout counter, at the moment untended. I walked down the housewares aisle to the knives. Half a dozen butcher knives, encased in plastic, were dangling from a metal bracket. This would have been where the murderer found his weapon.

I was standing at the butter end of the housewares aisle, sketching a quick map in my notebook, when I heard the swinging doors of the produce room burst open and turned in that direction to see Mark Hanlon pushing his way through, wearing a large apron with bits of green clinging to it and carrying a cardboard box of iceberg lettuce. I called out to him. He stopped and stared at me as I approached, holding the clumsy load awkwardly against his midsection.

"Hi, Mark. How are you?"

"I'm okay. I have to put these out." He jerked his chin down toward the lettuce.

"Of course. Go ahead."

"Thanks." He attempted a smile. "See you later."

"Exactly what time did we decide on?" I asked, following him. We hadn't been specific and I wanted to be, despite Tito's advice about appointments. Mark was acting awfully slippery; maybe pinning him down would degrease him a bit. Which thought reminded me of my sink and the dish soap I'd forgotten to buy over the weekend. Well, I was in a store. As Gilda would say, I could kill two puppy-mill owners with one stone.

He began taking the lettuces out of the box, placing them neatly in a well-cleaned space in the bins.

"I usually get off work at nine, but sometimes I have to stay late, so I can't say for sure." He had that edge to his voice, that I'm-trying-to-be-patient-with-this-pest tone.

"I'll be at your house at nine-fifteen."

Mark dropped a lettuce on the floor, picked it up, put it aside, all without looking at me, and went on stocking the bin. "Okay." I left him alone.

The manager's office was tucked into a corner up near the entry. I could see him sitting in there through the little wire-meshed window in the door. I knocked. He looked up from some papers, smiled, hopped out of his seat, and let me in. A cozy little closet, with a desk, two chairs, one four-drawer file cabinet, and not quite enough room left over for one person to do low-impact aerobics.

"What a very real pleasure to see you again, Ms. Lake," he crooned, waving me toward the grubby little pea-green molded plastic chair that huddled beside his desk.

I sat. He leaned back in his own swivel chair and smiled at me with his damp red lips, smoothing back his dark oiled hair. His face looked even shinier and redder than it had the day before.

"Now, exactly where do you want to start?"

First, I told him, I needed copies of whatever worksheets he had for the night of Anderson's death: who was on, who was off, who was assigned to what. Then I wanted the names of any employees who might have seen anything of what happened.

"The police have all that," he said, smiling.

I smiled back. "But I don't." He nodded, went to the file cabinet, searched for a moment, and pulled out some papers. Then he crossed to the door of his office and called over a young woman clerk who had just finished bagging a cartful of groceries.

"One copy of each," he told the clerk brusquely. She trotted off.

He sat down again, the smile stuck back on. "Nobody saw the murder, as I'm sure you'll find out. None of my employees, anyway. Now, what else can I do for you?"

"Tell me about Jane Wahlman, Mr. Borden. She

was here the night her teacher was killed. How can you be sure she—or anyone else—didn't see it happen?''

He thought, pulling at an already pendulous earlobe.

''Well . . . I suppose I *can't* be sure, now that you mention it. But basically everyone said they didn't see it—my people, that is, and everyone else the police questioned.''

I decided to get back to that later. I wanted him to get past what people had said to the police, to get down to how they had looked and acted. But first I wanted to know more about Jane, or, rather, his take on her.

''What was Jane like as an employee? Was she a good worker? Did she get along with the other people here?''

Borden nodded again. ''Basically she's a nice enough kid. Pretty good worker. Not dedicated, you know. Not career or anything, but a good kid.''

''And did she get along? Any special friends here, anyone she had problems with?''

''You know her boyfriend works here, I guess?''

''Yes. Mark Hanlon. Was that ever a problem?''

He nodded and grinned. The nod, apparently, meant as little as the smile. ''You mean hanky-panky in the meat department?''

''No, that wasn't exactly what I had in mind.''

''Well, basically they behaved pretty well here, for kids. Talked to each other a little too much sometimes when they should have been working. That kind of thing.''

"What about when they were arguing?"

He thought for a moment, snapping his thumbnail between his front teeth. Then he removed his thumb from his mouth and smiled and nodded again. He reminded me of a ventriloquist's dummy. "I wouldn't say they ever had a real knock-down-drag-out here or anything. Sometimes you could see they were talking to each other in a serious way, like maybe they had some trouble. But I try to stay out of my employees' lives. Barely have time for my own since the divorce." He winked. The office seemed to be shrinking.

"Did anything like that happen right before she disappeared?"

He nodded. "Well, you know, a couple of days before she didn't come back, I do remember them having some kind of discussion, on a break, standing out back. Not loud. But Mark looked a little, well, maybe upset, I thought."

"Do you remember what day that was?"

He looked at a calendar. "Tuesday. The 20th I'd say."

She'd taken off the next day.

"And how did she look?"

He smiled. "I don't remember, exactly." He paused and looked thoughtful. "Serious. kind of intense. But she got that way sometimes."

"So she was often serious and intense?"

"I don't know, she was just kind of like that, basically. You know?"

"What about real unhappiness—did you ever see that? Any clues that she was unhappy, at

home, school, or here at work? Did you have any
clue that she might suddenly take off? Anything
she might have said?"

He smiled. Why, I wondered, does this man
keep smiling? "No. Basically, she seemed okay.
Maybe a little quiet lately, but you work with kids,
you try not to notice their moods too much. Drive
you nuts." He laughed.

"She didn't give you notice or anything, just
stopped showing up?"

"That's right. One day she was here, next day
she wasn't. But you get used to that. Say"—he
leaned toward me slightly—"how's a girl like
you—guess I should say 'woman'—get into this
private-eye work?"

"It isn't easy." That was a lie. Getting into it
had been very easy. Actually doing it might be
something else again. If this man smiled, nodded,
played with part of his face, or said "basically"
one more time, I wasn't sure I could be responsible for my actions—or my words.

"I wonder if you would describe to me what
happened on the night of William Anderson's
death? The whole scene—how the body was
found, who found it, who said and did what, who
showed up when?"

"It was terrible. Really terrible. Scared the heck
out of everybody. Really bad for business, too—
not that I'm saying that's the most important
thing, but hey, things were a little rough for a
while. Still not right. This isn't the kind of neighborhood where people take that kind of thing, you
know, for granted."

"I understand. From what you said yesterday, it must have been nightmarish."

He nodded, remembering. He looked more sulky than sober. Then he smiled again.

"You want me to describe everything to you—better than yesterday?"

"Yes, please."

"Okay. Let's do it right. Let's go right over to the scene of the crime, as they say."

He opened the office door for me and guided me through, his fingers just touching my elbow. I could feel the hair standing up on my arm, but more than anything, I was relieved to escape that tight little office.

"I was manning one of the registers. It was a Thursday night, around nine. Real quiet, hardly anybody in the place. Then all of a sudden, there was this scream. Some woman. Real loud. Coming from cereal. Now that's who the police need to find. That woman. I started to run—some of the clerks did, too, and I had to make sure people stayed where they belonged and stood by their registers."

The general deploying his troops, I thought.

We reached the cereal aisle. Borden led me beyond the Sugar Pops and Froot Loops to the Nature's Own Granola end of it.

"Anyway, this woman comes running out of the aisle and before anyone can stop her—she's screaming like a maniac—she's out the door. A couple of customers beat me to the scene. A couple of employees were there ahead of me, too. What I saw was really something.

"Here's this guy. He was wearing white running shorts, but like I told you yesterday they weren't white anymore, if you know what I mean. And he was laying here on the floor, next to a shopping cart with a few things in it. And all over the place was this cereal. He was laying in it, it was all over stuck to the floor where the guy had bled." He grabbed a box off the shelf. "It was this stuff." He held it up in front of my face. Some kind of corn bran. "Little yellow pillow-shaped things, all over the place." The picture on the box did, indeed, show little yellow pillow-shaped things. They had not been part of his shorter account the day before—that had concentrated entirely on the gore.

"And here's this bloody scrap of a cereal box pinned to his chest like some kind of sign, pinned to his chest with one of our own butcher knives. I'm telling you, there was cereal everywhere, and blood. And nobody to say what happened." He pointed down to the end of the aisle, to the express checkout. "That checkout wasn't open. And on top of everything else, the cops wouldn't let me clean up the mess for hours."

Borden was telling the story with more wonder than horror, as though he'd felt no pity at all. I suppose I thought someone should. For a few moments I took on the burden, trying to feel Anderson's shock and fear—did he know his attacker?—trying to see his death the way it had happened, through his eyes, through his pain. I saw the knife coming toward me, and that was when I shook off the vision. I was not obligated to conduct my own little memorial service here in the supermarket aisle. He was dead, I hadn't liked him, and I couldn't "see" anything I didn't already know, like the face of his killer.

"Jane was working that night, wasn't she? And Mark?"

"Yes indeed. They saw him laying there. I knew it was someone Jane knew, I'd seen her talking to him once or twice. Mark said it was their teacher." And according to the information Tito had gotten, none of the employees—or anyone else still in the store when the police got there—had been splattered with blood. There had been a few smears on the floor, a few drops leading in the direction of the produce room, but no clear bloody footprints near the body, no bloody clothes found nearby.

I checked Borden out on those points, and he confirmed them.

"I'd of noticed if someone—besides the corpse—had been bloodied up," he said. "It just wasn't that way. Of course, I didn't get a great look at that woman that ran out screaming, but nobody noticed blood on her."

"And besides, what little trail the killer left seemed to be heading in another direction, right?"

"Right."

"If the killer got out of the store, how do you think he did that without being seen?"

"Oh, he got out, all right. Out through the produce room. The loading dock was locked, but the back door wasn't, yet. And no one would of seen him run through, because I didn't have anyone working produce that close to closing. I was about to go and lock it up myself when I heard the scream."

He laughed. "If I'd gotten back there a few minutes earlier, I guess I could of been a hero, huh? Caught the killer?" He shook his head ruefully.

"Or gotten killed," I said.

He shook his head again. And smiled.

"Listen, would it be okay if I kind of did a couple of things while we talked? You know how it is. Gotta keep an eye on people."

The request sounded reasonable. "I guess so."

He took off at a fast walk down the aisle, waving me after him. I caught up just as he was turning right to race along the bank of registers to the far side of the store.

"Tell me more about how Jane acted that night. Did she get to the scene ahead of you? Did Mark?"

"No, I'm pretty sure it was just the people I told the police about—a couple employees, a couple customers—but you know, I mean, things were pretty wild there for a few minutes, people rushing around. Basically what you remember is impressions. If someone was standing where I couldn't see him . . . well, I didn't see him. And it got crowded pretty fast—must of been a dozen or more people jammed in there. Everyone that was in the store except for the clerks at their registers. I mean, that's not a lot of people to be in the store, but you know what I mean."

"And you're pretty sure you didn't see Jane or Mark when you first got there?"

"I looked up to see who I could send to the phone to call 911, and I remember seeing Jane come up behind someone. She took one look at the body and started crying. Course, other people were carrying on too, getting sick, you know, but that was when I realized the guy was the same guy I'd seen her talking to. Didn't register right away, you know, you see a guy all messed up like that, he doesn't look the same as clean and on his feet."

"And alive."

"Yeah. Alive."

"Could you give me the names of those people, the ones you think were first at the scene?" I asked. He recited four names, the same names Tito had. According to his information, they'd all been dead ends. Maybe I'd need to check them again. Maybe not.

Borden stopped at the meat department, held up his hand to indicate a halt in the interview, and raced down the length of the counter and back again, a critical eye sizing up the packages.

"I'll be right back," he said, smiling, and disappeared into the meat-cutting room. I heard his unpleasantly raised voice, briefly, something about ground beef, before he reappeared.

"You got to watch them every minute." He stuck out his chest and led me off toward the back of the store, past the ends of two or three aisles, and into frozen foods.

A young woman was stacking frozen dinners in the upright freezers.

"I'm glad you're finally getting to that," Borden said sharply. "The Weight Watchers' was all messed up."

He started to move along the aisle again. I did not race after him. I had seen enough of his performance.

"Mr. Borden!"

He looked back, surprised.

"Stop right where you are." He stopped. I walked with reasonable speed to his side. "I would like, without interruption, to ask you one or two more questions, get the paperwork I need, and leave you to your job."

He laughed, and leaned back against a freezer full of pies. "Guess I move a little too fast for you. Moving fast—that's a big part of this job. You're going to have to learn to keep up."

This guy really had a smooth line. I was betting that all the women he flirted with this way just fell right into his arms. I had a moment's image of one of the lemon meringues smeared across his grin, but I thought better of it. The pies were frozen and probably wouldn't smear.

"Okay, now, how about I check one more thing, then I meet you back at my office in"—he looked at his watch—"three minutes?"

"Fine," I said agreeably. I was thinking of Borden colliding with a rock-hard Boston cream. "There are a couple of things I want to pick up."

"You're going to shop?" He was delighted. I was not happy to have delighted him.

As I picked up a bottle of dish soap, I noticed that Mark was working at the end of the aisle, doing something with the sponges. I caught his eye. He nodded, then bustled off somewhere else. I found a box of my favorite laundry detergent, if there could be such a thing, and turned in the direction of the express registers.

I went to the end of the short line. Mark, like Borden, seemed to move around the store fast. He was now bagging, one register away. While the clerk was ringing up my purchases, Mark came over to bag them. He nodded at me again, put the bag in a cart, and moved back to the other register.

Just as I was getting my change, Borden trotted up with a sheaf of papers in his hand.

"There you are! Just come on back to my office when you're ready."

The thought of squeezing into that tiny office with him again was suddenly too much.

"I've got only a couple more questions. How about walking me out to my car instead?"

He loved the idea.

"I'll just put these in the bag," he said.

He slid the papers in and yanked the bag out of the cart. As we crossed to the section of parking lot where I'd left my car, I asked Borden whether he remembered seeing Jane anywhere or with anyone in particular just before the screaming woman announced the murder. He didn't.

"You think she did it?" His red face was avid.

"No, of course not." I remembered a question he hadn't really answered. "And besides Mark, was Jane close with any of the other employees?"

"Not that I ever noticed. Just Mark I think. Who *do* you think did it? Just between you and I?"

"Between you and *me*," I said with teacherly snottiness, "I have no idea. Was there anyone she especially didn't get along with?"

"Not that I ever noticed. Hey, what about the girl? You think she's dead or something? Why is everyone suddenly so interested?"

"I'm afraid I can't speculate. I'm sure you understand." I was sure he didn't, but, as I knew he would, he nodded and smiled.

We reached the car. "Sporty," he said approvingly. "I love these little babies. Just right for a private eye. Maybe I should get me one, you know, for hot dates."

Ignoring his gambit, I opened the hatch and he placed the bag inside.

"You like this work, this private-eye stuff? Driving around in a hot sports car all day?"

"Love it." Maybe it wouldn't be so hard to give up the RX7 after all.

I closed the hatch. "I get to meet the most interesting people."

His red face got a little redder, his red smile got wider, and he nodded. "I can imagine."

I thanked him and said I might want to talk to him again.

"I would be delighted," he said, gazed at me appraisingly for a moment, smiled, turned, and marched back toward the store entrance.

There was plenty of time before my appointment with Jane's stepfather. I decided to go home, check my answering machine, and heat up a can of chili.

I found a folded-over note taped to my front door,

a card in a stampless envelope in the mailbox, and two messages on the answering machine.

The first message was from my old pal Judy Cohen, calling to confirm that our next Plymouth Avenue Expatriates dinner was set for the twenty-third, at a restaurant across the bay in Marin County.

The idea for the Plymouth Avenue Expatriates dinners first came up at a twentieth high school reunion in Minneapolis. Six of us discovered that we all lived in or reasonably near the San Francisco Bay Area. Since then, and it's been several years now, we've been meeting every month for dinner. Spouses, partners, or dates are not allowed.

The old neighborhood really stays in the blood.

The second message was from Charlie, the young Marlon Brando.

"Hi, Barrett, where are you keeping yourself? Call me if you're free Thursday. I've got tickets to the Shaw play at the Berkeley Rep and I'd like to take you. Now read my card."

I carried the grocery bag, note, and card into the kitchen, set them on the table, filled the teakettle, put it on the stove, and sat down.

The note was from Gilda. It read,

"Hi! How's it going, shamus? Having fun? How about a movie? Not tonight, I've got my potluck. But tomorrow or Thursday? If I don't hear from you I'll assume you don't have the time."

Gilda's over-sixty singles group meets weekly to share a vegetarian dinner they are convinced will help them to live forever. Maybe it's working. Some of them are very old.

I would find some time, somewhere, to at least fill her in on what was going on.

Charlie's card was one of those blank, write-your-own-message kind. On the front was a simple, stylized line drawing of a rose with a bee resting on one petal. The message: "I have plans for you." I would definitely try to find the time for Charlie. After all, wasn't that kind of thing traditional for PI's? Even in the middle of a case?

I called and left a message on his machine—wondering for just a half-second where he might be—that I would try to break loose for Thursday but would call him Wednesday to confirm.

Then, finally, I reached into the grocery bag and pulled out the worksheets Borden had given me. Jane, it turned out, had been working all over the store that night. She'd been in produce early on, with a couple of stints at bagging, and time at the freezers. She'd even done some stocking in housewares. The sheets didn't say if she'd been hanging butcher knives. Mark's pattern wasn't much different, except he'd spent more time bagging. I couldn't find anyone who would have been at the cereal aisle when Anderson was killed.

Jane, Jane, Jane . . . what happened to you, and where have you gone?

I wanted my tea, but I'd filled the kettle too full and it wasn't whistling yet. I stood, reached inside the grocery bag, and pulled out the detergent box. When I stuck my hand in again, deeper, to grasp the dish soap lying on its side in the bottom, several small objects slid away from my fingers. I yanked the plastic bottle out and looked down into the bag. Lying on the bottom were a handful of little, yellow, pillow-shaped bits of corn bran cereal.

The teakettle started to scream.

13

I turned off the teakettle.

I made a cup of tea.

I massaged the pulse pounding in my temple, breathed deeply, sat down at the table, and began to drink the tea.

All right, I told myself. Calm down.

My first sight of the damned things had brought a panicky rush. They represented Anderson's violent death. They represented the chaos strewn by his killer, the lethal knife . . . these were the images they brought.

They scared the piss out of me.

But as I sat there, drinking tea, breathing deeply, thinking about my visit to the market, the fear gave way to a calm that in turn gave way to a slow-surfacing rage.

Only two people had had the opportunity to plant the cereal in the bag: Mark and Borden. So which one was it? Which one of those two bastards had pulled this nasty prank? And what was the object? Was it a threat, or a cute little joke? Either way, for just an instant, the culprit had achieved the reaction he'd wanted. Either way, I was not happy.

By the time I had finished my tea, I realized I no longer wanted to sit and seethe. I no longer wanted a can of chili. I wanted a confession.

Fifteen minutes later I was stalking the Savemor's aisles again, this time looking for Mark. I found him still in produce, culling bad bananas.

"Did you put the corn bran in my bag, Mark?"

His mouth dropped open, ruining his looks. "What are you doing back here?" he asked, before his manners caught up with him.

"I came back here to ask you if you put the corn bran in my bag."

He peered at me, shrugged, put down a brown banana, and crossed his arms over his chest self-protectively.

"Look, Ms. Lake, I don't remember what you bought. If you bought cereal, I bagged it."

"Not a box of cereal, Mark. A handful of corn bran. Just like the corn bran that William Anderson was lying in."

He glared at me suspiciously, as if he thought I might be lying. Then, his arms still crossed, he shook his head emphatically.

"Well, what kind of stupid thing . . . Look, if somebody put a handful of cereal in your bag for some reason, it sure wasn't me. And you don't have any good reason to think it was!"

Indignation is an easy act for most adolescents. Still, I was pretty well convinced by now that he was innocent—at least of the bran trick. As a threat it was subtle, and I was beginning to think Mark lacked subtlety. And if it were only a joke? Well, if he had any sense of humor at all I hadn't seen evidence of it lately.

I gave him back suspicious look for suspicious look and went off to find the other suspect.

Borden was in his office. He smiled when he saw me. A big, horse-toothed grin.

"Not a funny joke, Mr. Borden."

"Joke?"

I just glared at him.

He laughed and raised his hands in surrender. "Okay. You're right. Maybe it wasn't so funny after all. But hey, it got your attention, didn't it?"

"Yes. It certainly did that." I wanted to call him an idiot, a moron, a cretinous ghoul. But I didn't. I might need him again before the case was done. "But if you want to get my attention, I would suggest you don't do it by wasting my time and my energy. I have other things to do, you know, besides stand around this place squeezing admissions of childishness out of you."

He sulked. "It was just a joke."

"I'll see you again, Mr. Borden."

He smiled and nodded, as though I were giving him a second chance—at what, for God's sake?— and I closed the door between us and left the store.

One advantage of being a male detective, I now understood, was that one did not have to suffer the strange sexual come-ons of even stranger men. I don't know what problems male detectives might have with that kind of harassment, but a female Borden was simply beyond my imagination. At any rate, having collected my confession and chastised the perpetrator, I was able to consider the possibility of something to eat. I drove to a University Avenue taqueria, where I dawdled over a burrito and a beer until it was time to go see Jane's stepfather.

14

Neil Clapton's real estate office was on a trendy stretch of San Pablo Avenue in North Berkeley.

San Pablo has to be the longest north-south street in the East Bay, cutting through Oakland, Berkeley, and several small cities to the north. It's wide and straight, arrowing from Oakland neighborhoods where prostitutes and refrigerators are both sold on the street, through Berkeley's full range of economic classes to the suburban-looking commercial districts of Albany and El Cerrito, and on to the working class towns of Richmond and San Pablo.

In North Berkeley rents are going up, and the street is spotted with good clothing shops—if you don't mind trading durability for style—and places that started out selling old windows and bathtubs and now sell brass faucets and marble sinks.

Clapton had a good-sized storefront with clean windows, and no one's name on the sign but his own.

I parked a couple of doors away and sat in my car, ten minutes early and needing time. This was not going to be easy. I hated him sight unseen, and you can't walk into a man's office radiating hate and expect him to talk to you, to be willing to help you do your job.

In my years as a teacher I had seen a lot of ugly things and heard of even more. Lots of minor crimes, one boy convicted of rape, another who had murdered a friend.

And there was no way to grow up in the store and not see things I didn't want to see, know things I should never have known. I would never forget the creepy Mr. Olafson, who had looked at me with wet eyes, who had tried to convince me to visit him at his house, and had touched me once, when I was ten, slid his hand partway down the back of my pants.

Mr. Olafson had a daughter my age who was always being punished for something and was rarely allowed to play with the other children, a quiet girl the other kids shied away from. I didn't quite understand what was going on. No one ever talked about Yvonne and her father, not the kids, not the adults. But on some primitive level I knew, and I hated him.

It was going to be hard to stifle the voice that kept saying, "This grown man raped a child, and he did it for years. And for years he abused her and hurt her in other ways, as well, to keep the secret."

Other people, I knew, had to stifle voices like that all the time: social workers and psychologists and attorneys. I just couldn't stop wondering how they were able to do it.

I locked the car, walked to the door of the office,

and glanced in the window. There were two desks, both empty. I pushed open the door and a bell attached to the frame announced my arrival.

He burst out of an inner office, smiling, hand extended.

"I guess you're the detective, right?"

"Barrett Lake. Yes."

"Neil Clapton. Call me Neil." His face was round and soft-looking, the features small, the eyes close-set. He had a too-full head of gray-blond hair, blow-dried, carefully combed, and showing vestigial sideburns.

His hand was still aimed at me. I touched it, briefly, with two fingers. A soft white hand, like Mr. Olafson's.

"Come on in, sit down—can I get you something to drink?" He led me into the inner office. It was furnished with a desk, a big executive swivel chair, a couple of visitor's chairs, a leather settee with a glass coffee table, a small cabinet, and an office-size refrigerator. A large, half-full ashtray squatted on the desk. The one window, behind Clapton's chair, was closed, and the room smelled of stale smoke.

Clapton was wearing a pastel green short-sleeved shirt, no tie, well-pressed slacks, and shiny new loafers with tassels. His belly was big enough to hang over his belt.

"Nothing, thanks." I took one of the visitor's chairs, wanting the expanse of desk between us. On the wall to my left was a large—twelve-by-eighteen—framed photograph, a family portrait:

Clapton, a woman in her late thirties, and two young boys. He noticed my interest.

"That's the wife." He leaned back in his executive swivel. "And the twins." The woman was pretty and delicate-looking, with light brown hair tortured into a curly but unfashionable permanent. The twins were about ten years old. They smiled sweetly into the camera.

"How long have you been married, Mr. Clapton?"

"Just two years, now."

"Nice family." I tried to smile. "Ready-made." I was thinking that he seemed to tend toward that kind. I couldn't help it: I had to wonder about his relationship with the boys. More thoughts to stifle. Better start talking.

I pulled my notebook and pen out of my jacket pocket. "Okay, then, let's just get right to it. When was the last time you saw Jane?"

"Mind if I smoke?" he asked. I thought of saying yes but I didn't really mind all that much, and I can't stand the self-righteous zealots who make excuses for crack addicts and harangue smokers in public places. And probably barbecue with petroleum-soaked charcoal every weekend.

"No. Go ahead. But would you mind cracking that window?"

He swung around, unsnapped a couple of locks, and pushed the sash up. The air was warm and smelled of grass pollen. "The wife keeps nagging at me to quit, but you know how it is. . . . Did you ever smoke?"

"Yes. I do know how it is. When was the last time you saw your stepdaughter?"

He lit the cigarette and inhaled, frowning slightly. "I was getting to that. See, I'm not really sure. It must have been oh, hell, maybe three-four months ago, I stopped by that store she worked at, just to say hello."

"Did you stop in to see her often?"

"Every once in a while, when I was in the neighborhood on business." Jane's mother had been right about one thing: She and her daughter had not been close. She seemed to think that Jane never saw her stepfather.

"So you saw her three or four months ago, at her job—for a few minutes?"

"Yes. Like I said. Just to say hello." He stubbed out his cigarette. "Hey, I know what you'd like." He got up and went to the refrigerator. It was filled with mixers—tomato juice, ginger ale, soda— and beer. I thought I even saw a bottle of wine.

I was pretty sure this was one man who could not possibly know what I liked, and I felt smug when he pulled out two bottles of a Canadian beer I had always thought should be marketed in specimen jars.

He opened the cabinet, which contained bottles of liquor and several kinds of glasses, grabbed a couple of beer steins, and returned to his chair. Lining up the bottles and glasses, he reached in a desk drawer, found an opener, and popped the tops. Then, with a flourish, he poured my beer and handed it to me across the desk. He waited for me to drink and express my appreciation.

When I simply said "Thank you" and set the stein on the desk, he shrugged and poured his own.

He sucked down half his beer and lit another cigarette.

"Now about your stepdaughter. How did she seem when you saw her? Happy? Depressed?" Wouldn't she be depressed, automatically, when her stepfather was around?

He thought about that. "Just the same as always. She was a kid. Kids are happy, right? What the heck have they got to worry about?" He chuckled, waiting for me to share the grown-up joke. I gazed back at him, expressionless, willing him to know what I knew about him and Jane, and the things she had once had to worry about. He stopped smiling and took a swig of beer.

"Anyway, she was busy, because she was at work. I said hello, she said hello, that was that."

"About how often did you stop by? To say hello?"

He frowned, then smiled a slight, ingratiating smile. "I told you. Once in a while." He leaned back as much as was possible in the swivel chair, knees wide apart, as though he were presenting his body to me. "What are you trying to ask me, anyway? I'm not sure I'm following you, here."

"I was just wondering how she felt about seeing you."

He took a swallow of beer, a hit of cigarette, and smiled boyishly. "What do you mean? How do you *think* she felt about seeing me?"

This was tiresome. "You know damned well what I mean."

He stopped smiling and sat forward, his hands hanging like claws between his knees. "Listen, I was the only father she knew for what, four-five years. She missed me."

"And you couldn't visit her at home, or have her at your house for an occasional weekend, I suppose."

He flushed. "No. And listen, I practically raised that kid. . . ."

"What did you talk about when you stopped by her job to say hello? What she was doing in school? Her dates? Your family? Her mother?" Did the girl tell him about her life, or did she just tell him to go away?

He shrugged. "Sure. All that kind of thing. I wanted to know how she was doing. You don't just forget a kid you raised." He wasn't looking at me: out the window, at the photo of his new family, at the ceiling.

I remembered Jane's father staring out the window, too. Funny thing. Even some of the people who were willing to talk to me wouldn't look at me.

"And she didn't forget you."

"Hell, no!"

I repeated my earlier question. "How did she feel about seeing you?"

"She was happy to see me." His eyes met mine, suddenly. They looked damp. His mouth was twisted. "She knows I love her."

He lit another cigarette. Despite the open window, I knew, the air in the room would be unbreathable soon. I coughed. He was still looking at me petulantly. He wasn't going to ask if the smoke was bothering me. He wasn't going to admit he noticed, or pretend he cared. Either I was being punished or he always pushed at other people's limits.

"I wonder if you could smoke a little less," I said.

He inclined his head in a parody of graciousness, and ground the fresh cigarette out in the mess in the ashtray.

"How did she feel when her mother threw you out, four years ago?"

"I don't know." He looked down at his hands, now clasped in his lap. "Confused, I guess."

"Confused?"

"Maybe sad. And glad, too. I was always the one who disciplined her." He said it softly, glancing quickly at me and then away again.

"If you thought she was glad to see you gone, why did you visit her at work?"

"I didn't make a big thing out of seeing her. I didn't try. I didn't want to deal with her dippy mother, for one thing. I didn't see her for two, three years. When I did, then she said it would be okay if I stopped by sometimes, there. At the SaveMor." He cast a defiant glare over his beer stein. "She said it was okay. I guess that would mean she wanted to see me, wouldn't it?"

"I don't know what it means."

He sighed, drained his glass, and shook his head sadly. "Listen, don't believe everything that mother of hers told you. I'm not such a bad guy. Better than some. Better than her own damn father. He practically abandoned her. Is he paying your tab?'' I didn't answer. ''Well, it's the least he can do.''

''If you never saw her, when did she tell you it would be okay for you to visit her at work?''

He shook his head and lit another cigarette. ''You could drink that beer, you know.'' I was hurting his feelings. He was misunderstood, misrepresented. He had never done anything Jane didn't want. I waited for him to answer my question.

''Okay, I was on the street, doing business, and stopped in for a six-pack. There she was. I didn't even know she worked there.''

''Why do you think she might have run away, Mr. Clapton?''

''Kids run away, don't they? You hear about it all the time. She probably had a fight with her mother.''

''Did they fight a lot?''

''Hell, how would I know? I didn't live there anymore, did I? But that mother of hers, well, she never understood Jane.''

That's true enough, I thought, but if I stayed much longer I was going to explode.

''So you think she's probably all right? Safe? that no one else had anything to do with her disappearance? That it's really voluntary?''

He slammed his palm down on the desk.

''Listen, if I thought she was in trouble, I'd be out there right now hunting!''

''And you can't think of any reason, anything she might have told you, why she might have gone? Was she in trouble at school, with a boy-friend?''

''No. She would just say she was okay, and how was I, and like that. But I guess maybe she wasn't so happy at home, or she wouldn't have run away.''

''Did she ever talk to you about anyplace she wanted to move to? Or even just visit?''

''You mean like a place she'd pick to run off to when she decided to run?'' I nodded. ''She never mentioned anyplace to me.''

I stood up, handing him an agency card with my name scribbled on it.

''Thanks for your help, Mr. Clapton. If I have more questions, I'll call you again.''

He walked me through the outer office to the front door and opened it for me.

''Nice meeting you, Ms. Lake.''

I turned to face him. I had to ask it. ''Does your current wife know why your first marriage ended?''

''You don't know anything about it,'' he said, ''and maybe you shouldn't judge what you don't know.''

''That may be. But if there's anything you think I don't know that will help me find Jane, give me a call.''

I could feel him watching me as I walked down the street. I unlocked my car door and looked back. He was still watching. He raised his hand in a wave. I got in, started the car, and drove away.

15

All the way to Mark's house, I thought about Jane's history with Clapton and how it must have affected her feelings about men.

I had known several women who had been forced into incest as children, and they weren't very much alike. Two of them wanted nothing, ever, to do with men, and had taken only women lovers. Another had continued to sell herself to men—her father had demanded "payment" for meals and ordinary privileges—until she was thirty, at which point she had a child, quit prostitution, and settled down to live in peaceful celibacy. The fourth had been a compulsive seducer and heartbreaker who was attracted to men—mostly men, at any rate—who looked like the uncle who had raped her. She was on her fourth husband, and I often wondered how much more punishment either of them could take.

Surely, I thought, there are also some who find a man they can trust, settle down and live more or less happily ever after.

So what was the story with Jane? What had she and Mark been like together? What had they been discussing so seriously the week she left? As much as I wanted to pursue Anderson's murder, Jane's disappearance was at least as likely to have something to do with her love life.

Mark's house, a large brown-shingle with a small, well-tended front yard, was on a comfortably middle-class street in Berkeley's Elmwood District, south of campus, one of those neighborhoods where homes have appreciated into the small-fortune range.

I rang the bell and an attractive, dark-haired, middle-aged woman came to the door. She was dressed in a full skirt, Birkenstock sandals, a bright flowered blouse, large red plastic hoop earrings, and multicolored plastic bracelets. Her hair was shoulder-length and curly. I thought she had probably lived in Berkeley since the Sixties and would never change her style. She squinted at me suspiciously—I could see her son in that look—but when I smiled she relaxed a bit and smiled back at me tentatively.

"I'm Barrett Lake, Ms. Hanlon, one of Mark's teachers."

"Really?" She looked puzzled. "Well . . . do come in, please."

She led me into a white-painted living room with a large brick fireplace, bright Southwest Indian rugs, bright Southwest Indian paintings on the walls, and white-painted wicker furniture with colorful flowered cushions that went well with her blouse.

"Did you call and leave a message that you were coming? Did someone know and not tell me?"

''Mark knew I was coming to visit him tonight. I'm sorry if he didn't let you know.''

She sighed. ''Oh, well . . . But you're here to see *him*, then.'' She seemed relieved I had not come to talk to her. ''Is everything all right at school?''

''Fine. Is he here?''

''No, but he should be home soon. Perhaps you'll tell me what this is about.'' She sat on the wicker settee; I chose the rocker, a comforting kind of chair. This had not been an easy day.

I was not eager to involve a third party in my business with Mark, but the woman sat there, anxious and expectant, until I admitted my visit had nothing to do with school and showed her the agency card. I explained that we were looking for Jane and hoped that Mark would be able to help us find her.

She became noticeably less friendly.

''I think Mark has already gone through more than enough. He's tired when he gets home from work. Is this really necessary?''

''Yes, I'm afraid it is. You say he's gone through more than enough. Precisely what do you mean by that?''

She shrugged largely, in continental fashion, with much waving of the hands. Her bracelets collided dully with each other. ''Oh, that damned girl. I'm sure Mark has no idea of where she's gone. He's been terribly distressed by her disappearance. Terribly. Enough to break your heart. And God knows I can't guess why. He wasn't all that happy when she was around. I think she had some emotional problems. I think he was really getting sick to death of her, but he just couldn't admit it." She took a breath. "I'm sorry for the girl, of course, whatever her problems were, but frankly, for his sake, I'm relieved that she's gone."

Quite a speech. I didn't think the woman was really trying to be helpful, she was complaining more than anything, but she'd given me a good jumping-off place for my conversation with Mark.

I was about to follow up on the "sick to death of her" part when Mark came in the front door.

His mother jumped to her feet. "Hi, Mark, how are you feeling? Can I get you something?"

I was beginning to be irritated by her intensity about Mark. She needed to diversify. Have another child. Date more. Get a dog.

"No thanks, Mom. Nothing."

She looked politely at me. I shook my head.

"Well, then I'll just leave you two in privacy." She left the room, pushing open a swinging door into the kitchen, glancing back once, nervously.

I'll be very surprised, I thought, if she doesn't listen at the door.

Where to start? Why not with the main question?

"Why did Jane leave, Mark? Where do you think she is now?"

He shook his head. He shrugged.

"What happened to her?"

"I don't know."

"She had some problems, didn't she? What exactly were they? Did she have a bad temper? Was she too shy, afraid of people? Did she live in a dream world? Did she have trouble being with you?" I knew I was overloading him with questions, but I wanted to shake him loose.

"Hey, she had her dreams. Everybody does. She wanted to be an actress. And we usually got along okay. Everybody has problems sometimes."

This kid, I thought, is really good at saying nothing. He could run for President.

"What are you hiding?"

"Jesus!" he exploded. Just as quickly, he appeared to regret it. "I'm sorry, but you know, you sound like some stupid movie!"

I was afraid he might be right about that. "Mark, she's your friend, your girlfriend. I'm trying to help her, and you're not helping me. You and Lorene both are keeping something from me, and I want to know what it is."

"Lorene? I don't know what Lorene knows or doesn't know. And the truth is, Jane didn't tell me where she was going or why. There really isn't too much point in your asking me about it."

"Do you think her leaving had something to do with problems at home? You've met her family, right? Her mother, anyway?"

"Yeah. I met her mother. She seemed okay, but Jane doesn't like her much. I met her stepfather, too. He came in to the market sometimes, and one night she introduced me to him. I never met her real father."

"How did she feel about her stepfather?"

"She didn't like him. She told me he messed

with her when she was a kid.'' He shook his head disgustedly.

''You say he came to the market sometimes—was he around a lot?''

''Nah.''

''When was the last time you saw him there?''

He thought. ''Couple weeks before Anderson got offed.''

''A couple of weeks?''

''Yeah.''

That didn't gibe with what Clapton had told me, but I didn't know how reliable Mark's memory of that time was. A lot had happened since.

''Let's get back to you and Jane. You said everybody has trouble sometimes. What kind of trouble? Were you tired of her? Tired of her problems? Had you fought over something, broken up?''

''No. I wasn't tired of anything!''

His voice cracked, his face was screwing up, showing signs of imminent eruption—tears or a temper tantrum.

''Mark, calm down. . . .''

''Don't tell me that! I hate it! You say all this crap to me and then you expect me to be calm! Why don't you just believe me?''

Because you're lying, I thought. But I didn't say it. I wasn't ready for him to go right through the ceiling. Not yet, anyway. So I changed the subject.

''What kind of car do you drive?'' And does it have pantyhose and a raincoat in the trunk?

''Datsun—'78. Why?''

"Where were you when William Anderson was killed, Mark?"

He stretched out his legs, spread his arms wide, encompassing the entire settee. He looked slightly more comfortable with this subject than with talk of Jane, but maybe that was because he'd had more practice with it.

"At the store, working. Why do you want to know that? What's it got to do with Jane?"

"I want to know where everyone was. But I know you were at the store. I want to know where in the store."

"You mean how close to the scene of the crime? I don't really remember. I'm a courtesy clerk. I'm all over the place. Produce, frozen foods, bagging, helping people load their cars."

I had not asked him for a job description, and I didn't want one.

"Maybe you could be a little more specific than that," I insisted. Don't people usually remember, vividly, where they were at the time of a disaster or a great act of violence? Or does that hold true only for earthquakes and the deaths of Presidents?

He rubbed his eyes, scratched his head. "Sure. I can tell you the same thing that I told the cops. I was definitely inside the store when that woman screamed and ran out. I mean I wasn't out on the lot collecting carts. And I was somewhere not too far away—maybe the freezers—when I heard someone call out for help. The guy who found the body, that was. Then I ran over there. Over to the cereal aisle. Borden was already there, and a few other people.''

''What about Jane?''

''I don't know where she was right away, but she came running, too. She got there after a bunch of people. After Borden. After me.''

''And Borden knew that you were acquainted with Anderson.''

''I don't know. He knew Jane was. He asked her. But she was pretty upset, she was crying, so I told him who it was. Why do you keep asking me about Anderson? I thought you were looking for Jane.'' He repeated his earlier question: ''What's this got to do with Jane?''

''I don't know. Maybe nothing. Do you think her disappearance could be connected with his murder?''

He bit his lip. ''Absolutely not.'' The answer was too pat, his expression too flat, for someone who had, just a few minutes ago, insisted he knew nothing at all. Once again, I found him hard to believe.

''Mark, I'm going to ask you again. You and Jane were seen having an intense discussion just the day before she left. Were you fighting? What was going on between you? What were you talking about?''

''I don't know who told you that, but we didn't have any fights. Everything was okay.'' He stood up.

I was not ready to leave.

''How did she treat you, Mark? Did she hurt you? Did you hurt her?''

"I don't want to talk to you anymore," he said. "You don't believe anything I say."

He marched into the kitchen, the door swinging shut behind him. I followed him partway, as far as the dining room, and stopped. I heard his mother's voice, soft, asking him something; he muttered a reply. I moved closer to the kitchen door. Heard him yank the phone receiver off the hook and punch mercilessly at the buttons. Before I could hear him say anything, his mother's footsteps sounded briskly in my direction.

I backed into the living room as she pushed through this door. She was saying, "I hope you're not going out again tonight."

She turned, saw me, stopped, and fluttered her thin hands in a small, helpless manner. "You're still here."

"I was just leaving. I guess he doesn't want to talk to me anymore."

"Yes, well, as you can see, Ms. Lake, this is very difficult for him. I don't really think he can help you."

"Probably not. Sorry I upset him. Have a nice evening."

I left quickly and drove my car around the corner, to where I could just see their front door.

Sure enough, despite his mother's futile hope that he would stay home, it was only five minutes before Mark came out the front door, looked around, and loped over to an old blue Datsun parked on the street. When he turned onto Ashby Avenue, I sped past his house and slid into the traffic three cars behind him.

I had no idea whether Mark had ever seen or noticed my car at school, or would recognize it if he saw it now. Tito's disapproval of red sports cars made more sense all the time, and I was wishing that I had already managed to find something less conspicuous to drive.

I kept telling myself that Rob hadn't spotted me, and neither would Mark. Fortunately, the Ashby traffic provided some camouflage, and I could only hope that Mark was no more accustomed than Rob was to checking his rearview mirror for a tail.

He continued straight west down Ashby and, after passing Shattuck, began to signal for a left turn. The light was just turning yellow at Adeline when he made his left. Two of the cars that had been between us zipped on down Ashby, the third, good citizen, stopped for the now red light. With me stuck behind him.

Willing to get a ticket but wanting to keep my distance anyway, I strained to watch Mark's car scoot off down Adeline and, just before he hit the curve that joins Adeline and MLK, the north-south lights at my intersection turned yellow, I goosed the good citizen with my horn, zipped around him on the wrong side of the street and into the turn, narrowly missing a huge station wagon going south on the yellow and earning a honk or two myself—as well as the gestures, unseen by me, that must have accompanied the honks.

Mark had gotten stopped by the light at MLK, and the traffic on Adeline was sparse, so I slowed down and made it through just as the light was going red again.

He turned right at the liquor store on the corner, the one with the big security gate and the social club in front. He stopped in front of the gray frame cottage. I pulled in behind a car parked at the curb, watching him cross the sidewalk and go up the steps. When the door closed behind him, I drove down the street and parked around the corner, just far enough so I could see down the walk.

And I waited. An hour and a half later, Mark came back out of Lorene's house and drove north and east again, with me trailing him all the way home.

On my way back to my own place I stopped at a liquor store and picked up the latest copy of the *East Bay Dealer*, one of those fat classified papers that specializes in used cars.

16

The phone rang thirty seconds after I walked into my living room. I considered letting it ring. It was late. I was tired and wanted to lie down in the dark and let my mind roam through the case.

But maybe duty was calling. Or Mark, or Lorene, with, finally, something to say. I picked up the receiver.

"There you are!" Gilda crowed. "I thought I heard your door close."

"Aren't you being just a little too alert?"

"It won't hurt me. I want to know what you're up to. The last time I saw you, you told me you were going to be a private eye. That was Sunday, and I haven't seen you since. This is Tuesday. I waited up. Come over here and talk. I'll heat some sake. If you're hungry I've got some leftover Thai."

Suddenly, I realized how much I wanted and needed to talk about the case with her. She was my best friend. She was wise, sometimes, when she wasn't too emotionally involved. I would tell Gilda all the things I'd learned about Jane Wahlman and William Anderson, about Mark and Lorene, about Jane's mother and father and stepfather and boss. She would marvel at my astounding adventures, tell me how clever and brave I was. She would soothe my doubts and feed me sake, and she bought only the best sake.

"Sounds great, but you can skip the food. I'll be right there."

"Good. I'll be in the kitchen. Use your key."

Frantic and Harvey met me at the door, goofy-happy to see me the way only dogs ever are. Genghis the tabby, who considered himself master of the house and chief greeter, gave me the silent meow and rubbed against my leg. Only one other feline seemed to be around—Franklin, the little black-and-white kitten I'd met on Sunday. He was hanging upside down from the bottom of the couch, murdering a loose thread.

Gilda appeared at the kitchen door, her gray braid flying.

"Sit down, sweetie. I'll bring the sake in."

She disappeared again. I sat, and Genghis jumped into my lap. He weighed eighteen pounds, only a few of them fat. I scratched behind his tattered ears. Genghis, like all Gilda's pets, was a rescue case. She'd had him for years. He'd been found, dehydrated and nearly starved, locked inside a tool shed. He'd been two years old then, homeless, unneutered, and bore the scars, physical and emotional, of many battles for survival. But Genghis was one of the lucky ones. He hadn't been so badly abused by humans that he could never trust one again.

Gilda belonged to an organization that provided foster homes for the abused and abandoned cats and dogs of the East Bay until permanent homes could be found. Often, the foster home and permanent home both had been hers. Now, including the kitten, the cat count was six.

She reappeared carrying the sake bottle and cups on a tray. The black-and-white fluffball attacked her ankles and then bounded off to bash up against Harvey, a calm, affectionate poodle mix, who began licking the kitten. Frantic, a golden retriever who had had a difficult and nearly fatal early life, finished chasing his tail and plunked himself down, panting, near Gilda.

"Now tell me," Gilda said.

"You won't believe some of it."

"Yes I will. I've lived in the Bay Area for thirty years, you know."

I began with a full description of Jane and her dismal family history. I described William Anderson's death, using my memory of Borden's narrative and Tito's notes. I told her about Jane's disappearance a couple of weeks after the murder, about the phony LA tip, about Mark and Lorene and their nervous, secretive behavior. About Rob Harwood and Elizabeth Anderson having lunch together as far away from school as they could get.

I even told her about Pissed-Off Purvis and his obvious dislike of Anderson.

Gilda was horrified by my tale of the pantyhose bandit, and cheered my reckless escape.

She couldn't get enough of Floyd Borden and his corn-bran games. We both wanted him to be guilty of something—anything that would require jail time.

I finished up with that very evening: my encounter with Mark and his mother, and Mark's flight to Lorene's house.

Gilda didn't let me down. Not only did she express all the appropriate emotions at all the right times, but she paid close attention and had some thoughts of her own to contribute.

"The mother's not really an idiot, you know," Gilda said. "Just self-centered to the point of complicity. It's enough to make you swim out to sea and join the whales."

"Not quite." The sake was beginning to warm the cold places in the corners of my spirit. "And the father's to blame, too. He just walked off and left her."

"Tell me more about the boyfriend."

"He seems scared and very, very distressed. I don't think he's telling me the truth, or telling everything he knows, but I don't think he's actually done anything wrong. I find it hard to believe he'd hurt Jane."

"You're pretty soft on him. He is the boyfriend, after all. And he's an adolescent male. Who do you think commits all the violent crime in this country? Not supermarket managers."

"I just don't think it's that easy."

"But you know he's hiding something. So's the friend—what's her name?"

"Lorene. And of course they are."

"But the most interesting thing you've mentioned is the lunch date—the teacher and the teacher's widow. That opens up all sorts of possibilities. Like insurance money, illicit romance, dark plots—all that wonderful *film noir* kind of thing. Does anyone in this story look like Alan Ladd?''

''Pissed-Off Purvis might, if he'd take a bath.''

''I think you should talk to him again, that Pissed-Off What's-His-Name. If he hated Anderson that much, he may know more about him than you do. People like knowing things about people they hate.''

The thought was not pleasant. ''He's just a hostile, obnoxious cretin.'' On the other hand, I was remembering what Tito had said about outsiders being good observers. If anyone was an outsider, it was Pissed-Off Purvis.

''Keep an open mind,'' Gilda said annoyingly. We finished the first small bottles of sake, and she went to warm some more.

I sat peacefully, thinking about Pissed-Off Purvis, dressed in a baggy double-breasted suit and fedora. Gilda returned and wrenched me back to reason.

''You know, the more I think about it the more I like Harwood and the widow as the killers. That would mean Jane's running away had nothing at all to do with the murder. And think about it— her mother's a princess, her boyfriend's a humorless, sulky hulk. . . .'' She repeated ''sulky hulk'' a few times, softly, enjoying the sound of it. ''Her boss leaves a snail trial and her stepfather, who she has every reason to hate, visits her at work. The child did not need a murdered teacher to send her off to Eugene or Eureka or wherever she's gone.

"You need to find out what happened between Jane and her boyfriend. I think the wretched little beast killed her. And if you want to catch Anderson's killer, too, you need to find out who was at the market that night."

"So far it's Borden, Jane, and Mark. And several other employees and a few customers, none of whom seem to have any connection with Anderson that the police are able to see. And the screaming woman, who hasn't been found."

"Maybe Purvis shops there."

"I can't even imagine Purvis shopping."

She laughed. "Tell me all about Tito Broz. When can I meet him?"

I gave her a lengthy description of Tito, his first appearance at my door, our dinner and his agreement to let me work for nothing on the case, the day I'd spent soaking up information and technique at his office.

"You like him."

"I do, but not like that."

"He's really letting you work on your own. A beginner. He must have faith in you."

"I guess so—but I'm kind of torn. I like working on my own. And the work is like nothing I've ever done—I think I actually have a talent for it. I speed through the day, high energy, total confidence, but when I finally get tired, like I am now, there's this fear. Not of the physical danger, exactly, it's just that, in a way, I wish I were getting more instruction. I don't want Jane shortchanged because I'm a rank amateur.''

Gilda nodded. ''Have you talked to Tito every day?''

''Pretty much.''

''Then don't worry about it. I'm sure he's paying attention. And you! You're having a great time. You're so excited about working on this case, so absorbed, so completely, totally, absolutely involved. More than you are about teaching.''

I was moved by some contrary impulse, and possibly sake-induced melancholy, to defend my previously chosen life's work, if only in a token way.

''It's summer. I'm temporarily burnt out. It's been a long year.''

''You haven't been happy.''

''Oh, Gilda, what's happy? Who's happy?''

''I am.''

''And you couldn't be happier?''

''Of course I could. I could be forty years old. I wouldn't mind that. Or I could have a date Saturday night with a man who looks like Cary Grant in his prime. I think you *are* tired. You're being silly.''

''You're right. And you're right about how much I'm enjoying this work. But I'm scared, too. There's so much at stake. Jane's life. Maybe mine, too.''

Gilda gazed at me affectionately. ''Yes, I can see that. You could get hurt.'' She looked into her sake cup and we both mused for a moment. Harvey lay at Gilda's feet, snoring, the kitten Franklin curled against his side.

Gilda looked up at me again.

"That was a depressing little interval, Lake. Let's snap out of it. You're not really going to get rid of your car, are you?"

"I have to do something, I guess. . . ." I didn't want to sell it at all.

She smiled. "You could paint it mud brown."

"No. I couldn't." That was absolutely the last thing I'd do.

17

The next morning I woke up with my head just a little the worse for wear and my mind fuzzy with the babbling conjecture of the night before.

If I'd had some idea that being an investigator meant dashing around waving figurative swords and tossing down imaginary gauntlets, all romance and swashbuckle—like a boxing match, perhaps, only less painful—that idea had been well shot down.

First of all, it was dangerous.

And second, master's degree and years of teaching notwithstanding, this was the toughest mental challenge I'd ever faced.

I made more coffee than usual, sat down for an hour's respite with my copy of the *East Bay Dealer*, and let my fingers do the driving.

The paper had a few pages of refrigerators and real estate at the beginning, and eighty pages of auto photos and descriptions. A lot of private parties, as well as dealers, advertised in it, and that's where the good buys could be had. I had first seen the RX7 in the *Dealer*, and fallen in love.

Sipping coffee, nibbling toast, turning pages.

A 1980 Dodge Omni for twenty-five hundred. "Won't last!" the ad said. I could believe that. But it had the right style—none. Trucks, wreckers . . . a Volkswagen Dasher. Ugh. Why in the name of God did they stop making bugs? As if in answer to my question, there appeared on the next page a '75 Super-Beetle with a bra.

I wouldn't buy a car from someone who would put a bra on it.

Jeeps. Vans. Porsches. I couldn't afford a Porsche, and I didn't think that was what Tito had in mind. Well, hell. I had no desire for a pickup truck. Lots of RX7s. I caught myself looking at a LeBaron convertible. Cute. And only sixteen thousand dollars. A 1984 Chevette. Cheap, but who cared? Buicks. Fords. Toyotas. There were plenty of cheap cars I could afford, including—and this was where my eyes kept wandering—those pretty little English sports jobs. What I'm looking for, I told myself, is a scabby sedan in the two to three thousand range if I don't want to sell the RX7, or a quiet, reliable sedan for around six if I do sell it. Maybe a jeep? Hadn't I just heard something about them rolling over at thirty mph? What if I had to chase someone? A 1978 Chevy Malibu wagon, only fifteen hundred. V8. The Classics/Hot Rods section. A 1950 Chevy, sitting on flat tires in tall weeds. Two thousand or best offer. A super-spiffy '68 Mustang convertible. More money than I had. A '53 Bel Air. A '57 Ford Victoria. Well, they were sedans.

Motorcycles. There was an idea. No one would ever notice me on a motorcycle.

Boats. And right in the middle of a page that included boats, trucks, and a gorgeous 1988 Corvette, a photo of a horse. "Arabian stallion, excellent breeding, winner of [etc.]. Must sell." Now there was an idea.

I circled a couple of cars, folded up the *Dealer*, and drank the rest of my coffee. I'd seen a few I needed to check on. Brown ones.

18

I spotted Lorene entering a student restroom before first-hour class and caught up with her just inside the door.

"Lorene!"

She swung around and saw me, but she didn't stop walking.

"Ms. Lake, I really have to . . . you know? She waved in the direction of the stalls.

"Go ahead," I told her. "I'll wait."

She went into one of the stalls. Three more girls came in, used the toilets, the mirrors. The bell rang. We were alone again. Still, Lorene did not come out. Okay, I thought, I can do it through the door.

"Lorene, I know Mark went to see you last night, right after I talked to him at his house. He was upset by my questions, he called you and dashed right over. What's that all about?"

"We're friends," she said, flushing the toilet. If she said anything else, the noise drowned it out. She pushed open the stall door, glanced at herself in the mirror, and headed for the exit.

"I have to get to my next class. I'm already late. And I have to pick up—"

"Don't worry about it. I'll give you a late pass. What did you two talk about? Why is he so scared? What's he done?"

Lorene bit her lip, shifted her weight from one leg to the other, and thought about her answer. "What makes you think he's done anything? And what makes you think I'd know if he had? I'm telling you, I don't know what he's done, if he's done anything." She looked desperately toward the door to freedom. "He didn't tell me about that. We talked about Jane. He's worried, and so am I, and we talked about it and tried to figure out how we could help you find her. I got to go."

She launched herself out into the hallway. My guess was that she would find Mark as quickly as she could and tell him I'd followed him to her house. If I could catch him before she did, he might, in casting desperately about for a way to explain, say something interesting. He was a slower thinker than Lorene.

Unfortunately, I didn't get a chance to see him until later that morning, in class. I asked him to come out in the hall with me.

"You have no right to keep harassing me this way," he said coldly. "I've told you everything I know."

"Which is nothing, right? Why did you go running to Lorene's last night? You're in on something together, aren't you?"

No surprise on his face at all, since, of course, Lorene had already talked to him.

"I needed someone to talk to. About Jane. We

were trying to figure out if we did know something, maybe. What we could do to help find Jane.''

''I'm glad you two got your story straight,'' I snapped. ''I'm touched by your concern with helping me, and I'll certainly let you know if there's anything you can do.'' I was getting tired of the game these two were playing with me, very tired. I had to think of a way to break at least one of them down.

I left a message on Tito's office machine, saying that I'd like to talk to him sometime that day. Maybe he'd see something I couldn't see, come up with something I was failing to do.

Meanwhile, it turned out that in the chaos of the second-to-the-last-day of school, I had an extra hour of free time. I took a long lunch hour and went looking for Jane's stepfather.

This time, there was a woman sitting at one of the outer office desks. She told me Mr. Clapton was out showing a house and wanted to know if someone else could help me.

''No. I need to talk to him. It's quite important.''

''All right, I'll just call his beeper. Where can he get back to you?''

''I'll be hard to reach—tell you what, I can just catch him where he's working. Do you have the address? It's about a present for his stepdaughter, you see.''

''Oh, yes.'' She smiled. ''Such a beautiful girl.''

The address was in Rockridge, a trendy section of Oakland that borders a trendy section of Berkeley. The house was a few blocks below the hilly part of the neighborhood, much of which had burned in a giant fire storm in the fall of 1991. It was a large stucco California bungalow with a front porch, a rock-garden front yard, and an oak entry door, standing open.

The hardwood floors reflected the glow of a single wall sconce. The kitchen light was on. I heard footsteps in there.

"Hello?" I called out.

Clapton came through the door with a puzzled look on his face, a look that went through several quick metamorphoses—surprise, irritation, resignation, and, finally, welcome.

"Looking for a house?"

"No. Looking for you. And here you are."

"Can't offer you a seat, there aren't any. How can I help you this time?"

I got right to the point. "You told me you hadn't seen Jane for two months before she took off. But somebody else has told me you were at the store just a couple of weeks before Anderson's murder. There seems to be a discrepancy."

He held up his hands. "Whoa, hold on! When was this guy killed again?"

"Two weeks—thirteen days—before Jane left."

"Okay, and you say I was there a couple of weeks before that. Two weeks and two weeks add up to a month. Maybe it was a month, and not two. What's the big deal?"

"I didn't say it was a big deal, but it seems to me you were trying to stretch the truth a bit."

He sighed. "I'm sorry if I got it mixed up, if I

misled you somehow. But you're not going to find Jane by landing on every little glitch in my overworked memory. I've got a lot of business on my mind these days."

"Can you explain why you said two months?"

"I don't know. Maybe I thought it was two months. Maybe I didn't want you to go running back to her mother saying I was always visiting Jane. That would be about all I'd need, for you to get her on my case. Listen, I was just on my way back to the office. Is there anything else you need?"

"Yes. Where were you the night Anderson was killed?"

"Jesus, who the hell remembers?" He was standing at the front door, waving me through. I joined him on the porch while he locked the door. "What was the date, anyway?"

I told him.

"April eighth." He thought a minute. "Out of town. Spring Break for the kids. Wife and I and the boys spent a few days up north, Calistoga, Mendocino. Little vacation. Okay?"

"Okay, but—"

He reached out to touch my arm. I yanked it back, a purely reflexive action, and he sighed again and dropped his hand.

"Sorry. I just wanted to say I really want you to find Jane. She's a good kid, but she's kind of crazy in some ways and I'd like to know she's doing all right." I started to speak again but he held up his hand. "No, wait. You've been listening to a lot of stories about me, I can see that. But you've got to remember her mother hates me.''

"Jane told people about you, too.''

"She followed her mother's lead. Don't ever forget, no one sent me to jail.''

"You're saying you never did any of the things Jane said you did? That it wasn't true that your wife found the two of you together and kicked you out?''

"Jane was a pretty messed-up kid. She was already a teenager by then, and she . . . well, she tempted me, or tried to, and got me into a situation that looked pretty compromising. I'm telling you this because I don't want you wasting time on me like this. I want you to know the truth.''

"So you're saying you were guilty only one time, or what?''

"Not as guilty as they say. Just guilty enough to feel really bad. Guilty inside. Guilty enough to give that damned woman a way to get back at me. I don't want to say anything bad about Jane. She's my kid. When you find her, you tell her if she needs anything, I'm here.'' His eyes glittered with tears. He turned away, pulled out a hanky, and blew his nose. "I've got to get back to the office.'' He stuffed the hanky in his pocket and glanced back at me, wiping a tear off his cheek with his hand. "Anything else you want to talk about?''

I felt disoriented. He still repelled me, but, now, so did my own hatred for him.

I had wanted to believe Clapton was a child-rapist, a bastard of the worst kind. My reaction to the stories had been instantaneous and outraged—the anger that nearly every woman carries, ready to ignite. An awful lot of us have known a Mr. Olafson.

And now, I found myself wanting to believe he was just a weak-willed asshole who'd had some trouble keeping it in his pants. One time. When tempted. Wanting to believe Jane had suffered less, and he was a human being.

Maybe, as a detective, I needed to keep a cooler and more skeptical head.

He was waiting for me to say something. I remembered what it was I had tried to say before.

"Are you sure you were out of town that night? Spring Break wasn't until the following week. Anderson was killed on a Thursday."

"Thursday? Well, just a second. That's wrong, then. We didn't actually leave until Friday, so that would have been the ninth."

He was smiling at me, as though he were pleased he'd recalled the truth.

"Then where were you Thursday night?"

"Home packing," he said, getting into his car.

On my way back to school I stopped at a pay phone and found Clapton's home phone number in the book. A woman answered.

"Is this Ms. Clapton?" I asked.

"Yes it is."

"My name is Greenly. I'm a client of your husband's."

"Oh, I'm afraid he isn't home. You can reach him at the office, though."

"I just called there. He's out. But I don't actually need to talk to him. This isn't about business.

He was telling me about some wonderful vacation spots your family visited in April and I'd like the names of the places you stayed—he said you had such a terrific time."

"Oh, yes." She sounded pleased. "We really did."

"Could you tell me a bit about it? We're going to be traveling up that way next month, and—"

"Of course. I'd be happy to help." She proceeded to rattle off a list of restaurants and inns, recommending a bed and breakfast in Jenner and one in Mendocino. I didn't bother to write down the names; they weren't what I was after.

"What a delightful trip!" I gushed. "How long were you gone?"

"Just a little over a week. The boys had to get back for school. We left on the Friday and returned the following Sunday night."

"That was Friday the ninth?"

She hesitated. I'd gone too far. "Yes. I believe so. Why do you ask?"

I ignored the question, gushed a little more, thanked her at least twice, and said good-bye. I wondered how Clapton would react to hearing that his client, Mrs. Greenly, had called. I could guess. No point in worrying about it, though. For all I knew he had a client by that name.

All that work and I'd only succeeded in proving that Clapton, along with everyone else, had indeed been in town on the eighth of April. Big deal.

I spent every spare minute for the rest of the day with my notes. I even drew a month-of-April calendar in my notebook, circling the date of the murder, the eighth, and the date of Jane's disappearance, Wednesday the twenty-first, as well as writing the words "Spring Break" across the week of the twelfth. I wondered how much contact Jane had had, that week, with the people she knew at school.

A few minutes before three, Tito stuck his head in my classroom door and winked at me. When the bell rang, he was waiting outside in the hall.

"You wanted to talk to me about something? Here I am, kiddo."

"Walk me out to my car. I've only got about fifteen minutes before I'm supposed to meet Harwood."

I filled him in to date, including my talk with Clapton, and Mark and Lorene's complicity in God knew what.

"Those two again. People won't talk, they won't talk. You have to get at them from another angle. See what they do. Get to the people close to them. Meanwhile, you've got other leads, other possibilities. You go for those."

"I thought I had something with the discrepancy in Clapton's story."

He shrugged. "You did what you could. That was nice work."

Nice but futile. "Thanks."

"Listen, you're doing a good job. Jest keep hammering away at it. You'll get a break. Now go land on this Harwood guy."

"Okay, coach."

I started to get into my car. He stopped me.

"Something I've been meaning to ask—about that suit of armor."

"Ivanhoe."

"Whatever, yeah. Well, I don't suppose you'd consider moving it into the office? It would look great. Impress clients. Very classy."

"No, I wouldn't. But I guess that means you want to keep me around?"

He grinned. "Don't make any assumptions."

19

Rob was sitting at the bar of the Elbow Room when I got there. He grabbed his red wine when he saw me, and waved me toward a booth.

"What are you drinking?" he asked as I sat down.

"Campari and soda with a twist. Tall." I was warm and thirsty and this was a drink with no punch—about as affecting as lemonade. He went to the bar, ordered my nice red glassful—it looked like strawberry soda pop—and brought it back.

"Thanks," I said. "But I should be buying. I'm the one who asked to talk to you."

He shrugged. "Get the next one. You want to chat about Jane, let's do it." He was tense, serious, and seemed to be bracing himself.

Jane was no longer the only person I wanted to talk to him about, but I wasn't sure which one was a more sensitive subject. I decided that as long as he had prepared himself to talk about Jane I should ask him about Elizabeth Anderson. It struck me, on making that decision, that I suddenly seemed to be an adversarial position with most of the people I talked to, always approaching with my fists up, dancing on the balls of my feet, floating like a butterfly. Now it was time to sting like a bee:

"I saw you and Elizabeth Anderson having lunch together yesterday, Rob."

His face went blank. An interesting pattern in human behavior, I thought. The blank look at the approach of danger. Don't people know that a completely empty face is more revealing than anger, or humor, or a stupid stare would be?

"What's your point, Barrett?"

"Well, you seem to have some kind of relationship. You looked awfully glad to see her."

"I didn't come here so you could pry into my private life." He was all bleeding dignity and offended righteousness.

"Yes, you did. You came here to talk to me about your relationship with Jane. Since I first approached you about that I've learned of another relationship you're involved in that might offer me some information about this case—it's a mess, you know, with Jane's disappearance and Anderson's death stuck onto the side. I have to follow where my nose leads me."

This was all true, and had the advantage of making me sound sincere, friendly, and unsuspicious. God, I thought, I'm getting so good at this. I felt a little sleazy.

He relaxed a bit.

"Well, there's certainly no connection between my friendship with Elizabeth and Jane running away. That's absurd. I can't even imagine how those things would connect." He laughed and shook his head, indicating in his patronizing way that he thought I was a pretty poor excuse for a detective. I felt less sleazy.

"There's a dozen different ways, Rob. If Jane thought she was in love with you and realized you were having an affair with someone else . . ." Someone else whose husband had been murdered, but I left that hanging in the air.

He flushed, opened his mouth, closed it again. I guessed he didn't know which part of my supposed theory to deny first.

"That's ridiculous." He laughed and shook his head again, but the gesture wasn't anywhere near as flawless as it had been the first time.

"What precisely," I asked, "is ridiculous?"

"All of it. Elizabeth and I are friends. We've been friends for a while. We got to talking at a faculty party once, discovered we had a common love of the theater. She'd even done some acting. Anderson couldn't have cared less. The few times he'd gone with her to plays, he fell asleep. Last year she had some health problems. The theater made her happy, took her mind off it. We went to a few shows together."

"And he didn't care?"

"No, he didn't."

"Rob, are you gay?"

He looked confused for a moment. "Because I like theater?"

"No, of course not. Because he didn't care if you went out with his wife."

"The answer's no. I'm not. But he didn't want

to go and it meant a lot to her. We're all grown-ups, after all."

Are we really? I wondered.

"So you're just friends?" Just like Mark and Lorene, I thought. Were any of them telling me the truth? Did I have to follow Rob around until I caught the two of them in bed together? And would that prove anything, anyway?

"Yes," he said shortly.

"Okay, let's talk about Jane."

"Fine, but what about Jane? And why do you want to talk to me?"

"I want to talk to you for two reasons. First of all, you are the adviser to her favorite and apparently only school activity. You may very well know her better than any of her other teachers, better in some ways than her friends. I would think that would be self-evident." I could be patronizing, too.

"And the other reason I want to talk to you is because you're afraid to talk about her."

"I'm not afraid. What makes you think that?" A light sheen of sweat covered his forehead. He was rolling the stem of his now empty wineglass between his thumb and forefinger. I didn't answer.

"Well?" he insisted.

I shrugged, laid-back and very, very cool. "Half the people I question about Jane break into a sweat at the sound of her name. If you don't all have different reasons, I'm going to start suspecting you of conspiracy to murder her and hide her body."

"Oh, sure," he said, smiling, undoubtedly relieved to hear that he wasn't the only one I'd caught sweating. "I always commit my murders with crowds of nervous people. Want another one yet?" I shook my head. He went to the bar to order another glass of wine.

"Who else?" he asked when he came back. "I mean, who acts nervous?"

"Her boyfriend and her best friend."

"Who are they?" I decided to let him ask a few questions, relax a bit more, drink more wine, maybe open up. Maybe blow it somehow. I gave him their names.

He nodded. "Sure. I've seen her with one or the other. I met Mark once. And Lorene's been in and out of the Mummers. Nice kid."

"So. Now tell me about Jane. What she was like in the club, what was your relationship with her?"

He focused on his wineglass. "I wish you wouldn't use that word 'relationship.' She really loved acting. More than most. And she's good at it. Very good. She could take a small part and polish it and make it shine."

He was mixing his tenses. Jane was present and no longer present, all at the same time.

"I was looking in the yearbook the other day. She wasn't exactly featured prominently in the section on the club."

He shook his head and looked sad. "I know. That's because she was never featured very prominently in a play."

"But you say she was good—by the way, what day does The Mummers Club meet?"

"Mondays." I wrote it down. "And yes, she was good. And she deserved some of the leads. But she always insisted she wasn't ready for parts that big. She was so damned, well, self-effacing. And old. She seemed old for her age, kind of out of place among the other kids."

I thought that her "oldness" probably had something to do with her early introduction to rotten adult behavior.

"So what is it about her that makes you sweat?"

He spilled a few drops of wine on the table, deliberately, and began to draw a liquid picture. It was either a tree or a nuclear explosion.

"Look, it isn't true. If you've heard something, it isn't true."

"Really? It isn't?" I didn't have the slightest idea of what he was talking about, but I'd finally found a vein. If he was a bleeder, I might really get something going.

"Really. Look, I know the kid had a crush on me, but I don't get off on that, on young girls." I sat, silent, waiting for him to fill the space. He did. "Of course it's tough, you know, when a good-looking girl flirts with you all the time. It's hard not to respond a little, to maybe smile at her more, or be aware of her too much."

"So maybe the other students were aware of what was going on?"

"That's the point! *Nothing* was going on. I don't know what they've been saying. I don't know what her boyfriend thinks, or Lorene. I don't know what stories may have circulated. But they're not true."

"I never heard any stories, Rob. I don't know if anyone else heard any, or if anyone thought anything about it." What I was saying, I knew, would be soothing to him. But the truth was, I was going to have to ask around. I was going to have to find out if anyone had thought anything about it. And that in itself might make people wonder. I'd have to be careful.

"Well, thank God for that," he said.

We chatted a bit more about Jane, nothing consequential. But I kept thinking about her, flirting with this older man. If she had. And I kept thinking it was possible. That a child trained to have sex with a grown man—if she had been—might well have been conditioned to act seductive with them. Or simply might have been too aware of them as sexual beings, aware enough to get their receptors buzzing.

Almost as an afterthought, I asked Rob Harwood where he lived. It turned out he had a condo in North Berkeley and sometimes shopped at the SaveMor.

I asked him what he was doing on the night Anderson was murdered. He laughed and said he didn't remember, and that he probably wasn't doing anything at all.

We finished our drinks, and I turned down his offer of a second. I wanted to squeeze in an hour or so of in-person and on-foot car-shopping that afternoon. It was a task I could not avoid forever, and, I thought, maybe it would clear my head a bit.

My first stop was a consignment lot near down-

town Berkeley, which handled only merchandise
left by private owners. Unlike most used car dealers they had an interesting, sometimes amazing,
variety—including custom-built cars that look like
they were designed by a committee. People like
to go there just to browse, and, as I had discovered the last time I went looking, it's not a bad
place to meet men.

But today I was all business. I started at the
north end of the lot and worked my way method-
ically along the rows.

A very old Jeep station wagon, dirty white, with
seats that looked like they'd eject through the
windshield if you stepped too hard on the brake.
Charming, and almost coachlike in its design.

A 1951 Oldsmobile. A newish Corvette. An old
Saab that was nondescript and cute all at the same
time, and only eight hundred dollars. Unfortunately, it was missing a few necessities, like a fully
functioning clutch.

There was the usual assortment of BMWs, two
RX7s, both newer than mine, a couple of Mercedes, a Volkswagen fastback, and a mess of Toyotas. The cars I liked were either expensive or held
together with staples and paper clips. Everything
else was boring, which was what I was supposed
to be looking for.

Ten minutes later I pulled up at used-auto row
on Broadway in Oakland, a long, solid block of
lots between Piedmont and 30th.

I met three very friendly, not too pushy salespeople and rejected a ten-thousand-dollar LeBaron and a number of rabbits, cougars, mustangs,

and other animals. At the fourth lot I was distracted for a few diverting minutes by a 1949 Hudson that was not running and belonged to the owner's brother, who was going to restore it "sometime."

The last lot I had time for—Empire Used Autos—had all the usual items, plus a lot of Camaros and one car that interested me very much. Not because I wanted to buy it, but because I thought it could be the car that had blocked my way at Lorene's Monday night. It was the right shape and the right color, but, unfortunately, all cars from the early Seventies look exactly alike to me, especially in the dark, so I didn't know what make I was looking for. This one was a Maverick, whatever that is, and it had the same scars I'd seen on the car that night: a sightly dented front fender and a scratch all along the door. It didn't have to be the right one, but it sure could be.

"Good afternoon, miss, you interested in taking a test drive?"

I looked him over. Youngish, maybe thirty, but already over his own particular hill. His blond hair was a bit too long. He had a slight potbelly and a puffy face.

"Actually, I'm interested in knowing where you got this car."

He backed up a step. "Why?"

What was the best way to handle this? I didn't know. "I think it might have belonged to a friend of mine, someone I haven't seen in a while."

A pretty pathetic gambit, and I earned a suspicious glare for it.

"Really," I insisted. "I'd like to get a line on him, if it's the same guy."

"Don't tell me, let me guess. You want to find him because he's inherited the Tribune Tower, right? Or the Bay Bridge. What are you, an ex-wife? A lawyer? Or maybe some kind of cop or something?"

"Kind of a cop," I admitted.

"Then let's see your ID."

I reached into my pocket for one of Tito's cards.

"We don't sell stolen cars here, you know. We get them all legitimate." He read the card, slowly.

"I'm not after a stolen car," I said. "We really are looking for a friend." I was not about to tell him that the friend and the possible previous owner of this car were not the same person.

"Maybe you should talk to the boss." He marched off to a little hut at the back of the lot and returned with a tall, thin gray-haired man who had my card in his hand.

"I'm Jack Calderini. How can I help you?"

I smiled and gave him the line about the friend.

He smiled back. "I don't think so," he said, stuffing the card back in my hand. "We got this automobile from the widow of a dead guy. An old dead guy."

"Could I see the paperwork?"

He frowned at me, thought for a minute, shrugged expansively. "Oh, what the hell. Come on."

I followed him back to the hut-office and up the wooden steps.

"Sit down. I'll look for it." He pawed through

his files for a good five minutes before he came up with the right one. "Here you go."

The previous owner of the car had sold it to Calderini, cheap, two weeks before. Long before I'd met my raincoated attacker.

I thanked the man.

"It's okay," he said. "But you owe me a favor. Never can tell when I'll need a favor from a private eye, right?" He grinned. I was betting the man drank Scotch in a place that reminded him of the bar in *Peter Gunn*.

I chuckled noncommittally and went home.

20

Following Tito's advice I had made no appointments for that evening, and I was glad of it. Any reluctance I'd had to interview Elizabeth Anderson, any excuse I might have made that she was irrelevant, was gone. Her husband's murder aside, she had a fairly longstanding and questionable tie to Rob Harwood, and so, in some way and to some degree, did Jane.

I didn't want to face her bereavement. I didn't want to poke and prod and open old wounds. But I had to tell myself that Jane was worth it, and that the need to know the truth was worth it. I suspected that my ambivalence was just something I'd learn to live with. If I wanted to sift through piles of emotional debris, I had to be willing to get some on me.

First, though, I had to call Charlie and let him know I hadn't forgotten our rain check.

"If you're free tonight," I told him, "I'd love to have dinner—but late? Around nine?"

"Late's good," he said cheerfully. "I'll bring my pajamas."

I knew he must have women trailing him

around, young and gorgeous ones at that. But still, he had the perfect foresight to be free later that evening. No questions, no recriminations. And the promise of good things to come. Was he really as perfect as he seemed to be? Not possible. He would actually bring pajamas, they would have bunny feet, and he wouldn't be doing it for a joke.

I stifled the pessimism of years and sat down at the kitchen table to spend an hour with my notes and a cup of coffee.

At the end of that time—forty-five minutes, actually—I was no surer about what I was going to say to Anderson's widow, but I did feel that I had sorted out some of the odds and ends of the case, or at least compartmentalized them.

Olivia, acting like she was breaking the Clerk's Code but was willing to do it in a good cause, had pulled the address from the school files and written it down for me. I had stuck it in my pocket without looking.

Reading it now, I saw that William Anderson had lived in North Berkeley, but some distance from the SaveMor. I knew the neighborhood. There was a large Safeway store near the house and a couple of smaller markets not far away.

So why did Anderson shop farther from home? Probably not significant, I told myself. I have often driven farther to a store I preferred. Well, not often, really. But sometimes.

The house was set back behind big trees and a six-foot redwood fence. It was large, shingled, and painted white, and looked shabby around the

edges, the shrubs untrimmed, a loose shingle
here, a cracked wooden step there. I rang the bell.

The woman who came to the door looked tired.
Her shoulders were hunched, her cardigan held
together at her chest with one hand. She was big
and blond and, I thought, pretty in a pale and
rustic way, like a character in an Ingmar Bergman
film. I had not seen her close up for more than a
year, and the changes in her life were drawn on
her face. Whatever I might suspect about her and
Rob, her husband's death seemed to have marked
her. She looked at me quizzically.

"Do you remember me, Ms. Anderson? I'm
Barrett Lake."

"Oh, yes. You're a teacher at Tech," she murmured distractedly. "Excuse me, I was just resting. Please come in." She led me to a large living
room with ordinary, comfortable furniture, and
motioned for me to sit down, still holding the cardigan together.

"As I said, I was resting. Just let me go put
myself together. I'll be right back."

Before I could tell her there was no need for her
to put herself together, whatever that meant, she
was gone.

I surveyed the room. On the mantel, several
photographs in frames. The Andersons' wed-
ding—she had been very beautiful in a high-
cheekboned, ice maiden kind of way; an old sepia
picture of someone's grandparents; another couple from a more recent past—probably, from the
look of them, Elizabeth Anderson's parents—the
woman in a pompadour and snood, with wedgies

on her feet, and the man in uniform; and stuck into a corner of the frame, a small but fairly recent snapshot of William and Elizabeth Anderson.

I put it in my pocket.

When she returned a couple of minutes later she was standing up straighter, looking more alert, and her cardigan hung loosely over her small breasts.

"What can I help you with, Barrett? Something about William, I suppose, some question at school?" She smiled a polite smile. "I'll unpuzzle it if I can."

"Well, not exactly, Ms. Anderson. I'm working with this man." I handed her the agency card. "We're trying to find a student who has run away. She was a student of William's and she worked at the SaveMor. She was there the night he died. Her name is Jane Wahlman. I wonder if he ever mentioned her to you."

"Call me Elizabeth, please. Jane Wahlman . . . No, the name doesn't sound familiar. But William rarely mentioned students by name. He didn't talk very much about school, really." She laughed lightly. "Or much of anything else, I'm afraid. First there was my illness, and then he seemed to have so many meetings and things. . . . Well, you know how it can be. Sometimes you sort of lose touch."

Ah yes, the illness. I didn't remember ever hearing anything about it at school, nothing, in fact, until Rob had mentioned it earlier that day.

"I'm sorry you've been ill. I only heard about

it today, as a matter of fact, from Rob Harwood. I hope it was nothing serious."

She dropped her eyes, so I couldn't see any reaction to Rob's name, and touched her chest gently. "Mastectomy. Bilateral. And then the chemotherapy, of course . . . They do that so much more often these days, you know." She smiled at me. "I'm fine now, but it was hard for a few months. And hard on William, for me to be so sick. I think he was relieved, sometimes, that he had so much work to do, that he could go into his study or go to a meeting." Her mouth twisted. Her words were kind, but I wasn't so sure about her thoughts.

Now I understood why her posture had changed so radically after she'd left the room and come back. She had put on her prostheses. I felt sick with pain for her—because she'd gone through hell, and because she was now ashamed of the way she looked without those lumps of foam or silicone. I thought kind thoughts about Rob Harwood. If they were more than friends, he was not as shallow as I had always believed he was.

"I'm so sorry," I said again. "I can't believe I would never have heard about something so serious. Surely the teachers would have gotten together to send flowers to the hospital, or—"

"It's all right, Barrett, really. William was very . . . private about it."

The man was even stranger and more antisocial than I'd thought.

"But Rob knew."

"Rob is my friend."

"And he never mentioned it to anyone at school?"

"I don't think he thought it was his place."

I could understand that.

"Are you all right now? Finished with treatment?"

"Yes, we think so. I'll go through reconstruction, of course. I don't really know when. I'm a little scared of more surgery. But you don't want to talk about this. I just told you to explain that I've been somewhat out of it—not very likely to know anything about any of William's students, more involved in getting well than in sharing his problems at work."

I thought it was interesting that she used the word "problems" instead of a more neutral word.

"So I imagine he was doing all the shopping for a while."

"Yes. I wasn't supposed to lift anything at first. And I was so tired. I'm much better now, of course. The surgery was way last September, and I finished the chemo in March. He kept doing the shopping for a while, though. I was still pretty low, and he seemed to enjoy it." For some reason, she laughed. "He went regularly, every week, on Thursday evenings—he said the store wasn't so crowded then."

"Had you always shopped at the SaveMor? I noticed there are stores closer by."

"I had always gone to the Safeway on Shattuck. But he preferred the SaveMor. Said the quality was better." She shrugged. "I never noticed a difference."

"You said he had a lot of meetings at school in the last few months. What kinds of meetings were they?"

"He mentioned something once about a curriculum meeting, but I don't really know. He had business interests, too, here and there." Her mouth twisted in that bitter way again and she smiled at me—an odd little smile, I thought. "And I wasn't up to asking."

"Do you have any idea why someone would have wanted to kill your husband, Elizabeth?"

She sighed. "No. He wasn't the world's best-liked man, or the most sociable. But as I told the police, I don't know of anyone who would want to kill him that way." She giggled. "We never had any children, so they didn't do it." I must have stared at her, because she waved her hand at me and added, "Just a joke, Barrett. When one has had a year like the one I've had, one needs to joke."

"When I was talking to Rob Harwood today, Elizabeth, I mentioned to him that I saw the two of you having lunch together yesterday. You say you're friends—do you see him often?"

She answered casually, but there was warmth in her voice.

"We're good friends, Barrett. He was very kind to me last year, through everything. We have the same interests. We have lunch sometimes, yes. Not often, but sometimes."

"Did he ever talk about his students with you—might he have mentioned Jane Wahlman?"

She shook her head. "Try as I might, I can't recall anyone ever mentioning that name to me."

"I was noticing your house needs a bit of work. Didn't William leave enough insurance to take care of things like that?" A million-dollar policy, maybe, that would have made his death look irresistibly profitable to a pair of lovers? Wasn't there a *noir* film like that, or maybe five of them?

She smiled, her tiniest smile yet. "William didn't believe in carrying a lot of extra insurance. But he left a bit of money. Despite my little joke about children who might want to kill him, despite his lack of sociability, William was a good husband, a good provider, as people used to say. I'm just not good at seeing to things like house repairs, I'm afraid. I never had to do it before. I suppose I'll learn." A small laugh. A shrug.

I stood. "I'm sorry to have disturbed you. If there's any way that I can be of help, please let me know."

She escorted me to the door. "That's very sweet, but I don't need help anymore. I'm really just fine."

Anderson, I thought as I drove away, had obviously been small comfort to his wife during her ordeal. And she didn't seem overcome with grief that he was gone.

Who can I talk to, I wondered, who might have observed the two of them together? Again I recalled Tito's words about outsiders, about how observant they could be. I thought of the ultimate outsider; the gas station he worked at was close by. Maybe he had filled the Anderson family tank once in a while, had seen Anderson with his wife, had noticed how they were. I turned right at University Avenue.

"Ms. Lake. Back again so soon? Been doing a lot of driving?" Pissed-Off Purvis leered at me.

I glanced around the station. One other car, and it was at the self-serve island.

"I saw some oil where I sometimes park. I wonder if you'd mind checking it for me."

If he was suspicious of my supposed helplessness, he didn't show it. He shrugged, pulled a dirty paper wipe out of his coverall pocket, and waited while I popped the hood.

Carefully, he cleaned off the dipstick, reinserted it, pulled it out again, and studied it. He shook his head, folded the hood prop down into its clamp, and dropped the hood.

"Your oil's fine."

"Thank you, Gerald." I hesitated, couldn't think of a smooth transition, and plunged ahead.

"Gerald, did William Anderson ever come in here?"

"No, not that I ever saw." So much for that idea. "And I gotta say, I'm just as glad."

"You really disliked him, didn't you?"

Purvis nodded. His eyes had gone wary. "Yeah. So what?"

"I was just curious."

"Funny thing to be curious about."

Apparently word had not spread all around

school—at least not as far outside the circle as Purvis.

"Okay, Gerald, I guess you haven't heard. I'm working with a private investigator, and we're looking into Jane Wahlman's disappearance."

His eyes widened, his jaw dropped. Then he caught himself, closed his mouth, and sneered at me.

"Oh, sure. You always did have a good sense of humor."

I decided to just let the comment go for the time being.

"So tell me, what was your problem with him?"

Purvis shook his head, amused but tolerant of this crazy woman, unable to check her own oil, who was playing some weird game with him.

"He was a . . ." Purvis was searching, I was sure, for a less-than-obscene word to describe his former teacher. Had he been told to watch his language at work? "He was a phony. A real slime."

"You had him in a class?"

"Yeah, senior English."

"So you were in his class with Jane Wahlman."

"Yeah. Like, you're serious about this sh—stuff, this private-eye thing!"

"Did you know Jane well?"

"I didn't know her at all." A car pulled in behind me at the pump. "Listen, you want to pull out of the way so I can take care of this guy?"

I started my engine and pulled across the lot to the pay phone, parked, and got out. I walked back to the full-service pumps just as Purvis was beginning to fill the customer's tank.

"Tell me more about Anderson. Did you dislike him because of the grades he gave you?"

"Christ. Why would I care about that? I was passing. That was all I cared about."

He walked to the front of the car and began washing the windshield. I followed him.

"Then what was it? Are you sure he didn't come in here for service, maybe just once, and give you a hard time?"

"You really a private eye?"

"Yes."

"You investigating his murder?"

"Not exactly."

"Well I never saw him, not on this side of the street anyway, and I didn't kill the son of a bitch." He went to the driver's side window and asked the customer if he wanted him to check under the hood. The man did.

The hood popped, Purvis yanked it up, propped it, and began rummaging under it. "This side of the street," he'd said. The other side—motels.

"Someone hated him enough to kill him. I want to know what reasons people had for hating him. It seems to me he was an ordinary, respectable, decent kind of man, and a good teacher." That's how he'd looked to the world, anyway. "And what do you mean about 'this side of the street'?"

The customer in the car was fiddling with his stereo, and seemed to be hearing nothing of our conversation. So many people are so oddly oblivious, I thought, to things outside of themselves—even just outside of their cars. I knew I'd overhear a conversation about a murder no matter what I was doing.

Purvis snorted and laughed bitterly. "I didn't hate him. I just thought he was a pig. He acted like other people were dirt. Well, he was the one who was dirt, phony bastard! Prissy-assed son of a bitch was messing around with his own students."

The customer in the car had heard that. He turned down his stereo and pretended not to be listening to us.

"Who?"

"Could have been twenty different girls."

He shopped inconveniently at the SaveMor. He was secretive about his private life and uncomfortable with his peers. He had a lot of "meetings." She flirted with older men.

"Was one of them Jane?"

Purvis took the customer's money. Reluctantly, the man turned the key in his ignition, put the car into gear, and pulled away.

"Yeah, I guess so."

"You guess so, or you know so?"

He looked insulted. "I know! There's a lot of stuff I know."

"How precisely do you know?"

He jerked his thumb toward the motel row across University Avenue.

"I work here nights, that's how. He liked The Cabana, right over there."

"You're sure about this?"

"Yeah. I saw his car over there a few times. A

couple of days—one night, too, but I couldn't see so clear—I saw Jane get out of it.''

''And Anderson?''

''I couldn't just stand around watching. I got to pump gas, you know. But it was his car, all right. I saw him get out of it other times.''

This could all be a figment of his overheated and aggrieved imagination. But he seemed to be telling his story carefully, not stretching what sounded like the truth.

''Why would a teacher use a motel across the street from a gas station where one of his students worked?''

Purvis snorted. ''This is where most of the motels are, unless he wanted to go out of town—or down on MacArthur.'' MacArthur, I thought? Not unless he was after crack, prostitutes, or cockroaches, none of which was probably his style. ''He never came in. He didn't know that I work here. And you know what? Even if he saw me here, he'd of looked right through me.''

''If you hate him so much, why didn't you tell the police about this after he got killed?''

He shrugged. ''I thought about it, but why would I? No point in getting all sucked up in that shit. Besides, whoever offed the son of a bitch did a good thing.''

''Why are you telling me, now?''

''Because you pulled my chain with that 'respectable and decent' crap. It makes me vomit, everybody talking about what a good guy he was, like they always do about dead people.''

Purvis had a redeeming quality after all: He hated hypocrisy. Passionately.

"Did a lot of other people know what Anderson was doing?"

"I never heard nobody say so. You couldn't tell from watching him in class."

"Or Jane?"

"You couldn't tell from watching her, either."

That isn't surprising, I thought. Jane was used to concealing things like that.

"Did Mark Hanlon know?"

Purvis shrugged. "I sure as hell didn't tell him."

Before I left the gas station I went to the phone booth and checked the book. William and Elizabeth Anderson were listed. I pulled out my notebook. Paper-clipped inside it was the scrap of paper I'd taken out of Jane's desk, the one with the anonymous phone number on it. They matched.

Guinevere. Jane's hero. The beautiful queen with two lovers, Arthur, the older man, and Lancelot, the young one.

I drove back to the Anderson house and rang the bell.

Elizabeth opened the door clutching her sweater again. She was yawning.

"Did I wake you? I'm sorry."

"No, no, I was just nodding off at the TV, you know how that is. But I would rather like to go to bed. Did you have another question?"

I stood there on her front porch, unsure of how to put the question. Finally I just said it.

"Elizabeth, did you ever have any reason to suspect that your husband might be having an affair?"

Her face went rigid around a cold smile. "An affair? Do you mean recently?"

Had he been doing it for years? "Yes. Recently. And did you ever think he might be attracted to some of his students?"

She frowned, and rubbed the line between her eyes. Then she rubbed her cheeks, as if she wanted to soften them.

"Did Jane Wahlman, the student I asked you about, ever call him here at home?"

"No. Of course not. And I don't know why you think she would. He was killed by a maniac. His murder had nothing to do with anything. He loved me. I loved him. We were together for fifteen years. Now I don't want to talk about it anymore. Good night, Barrett." She closed the door gently in my face.

21

I sat in my car for a few minutes, debating my next move. I had Elizabeth Anderson's photo now, as well as the yearbook, with all those shots of Rob Harwood. Maybe Borden or one of his employees had spotted one or both of them at the market doing something interesting.

But questioning everyone at the market would take a lot of time, and I also really wanted to talk to Lorene. There was no way she was going to convince me she hadn't known anything about Jane and Anderson, hadn't been aware of a big problem between Jane and Mark. The next time I went looking for Mark I wanted to be carrying something that might cut through his armor, and it seemed to me that Lorene could give me that weapon.

The streetlights had just flickered on as I turned down a narrow side street on my way west to MLK Boulevard. When I was a little kid I had been amazed by that phenomenon. I wondered for months how the lights knew it was getting dark outside, and was disappointed when my mother explained in a vague kind of way—she never was very sure about how these things worked—that people turned the lights on somewhere downtown. A big switch, she said. Years later, when I saw Chaplin's *Modern Times*, I was reminded of that enormous switch I'd pictured in my imagination.

I was still several blocks from MLK when I noticed that the same car had been right behind me for a while, maybe even since I'd turned off Shattuck. It was a large old American car, a different color, brown, and a slightly different shape than the one I'd encountered outside Lorene's house, but just as nondescript and from the same era of big dumb cars. As I watched in my rearview mirror, it came within five feet of my Mazda's rear end. I slowed down to try to get a look at the driver's face and the license plate. He, or she, didn't honk, which would have been a normal response to my blocking the way. My stomach dropped, my heart began to pound in my ears. I could almost feel the adrenaline dumping into my bloodstream. My hands, on the wheel, were damp and wanted to cut loose and shake. I held on. I couldn't see him clearly. The front license plate was unreadable, smeared with some black gunk or other. I could just make out a two and an A, several spaces apart. Gritting my teeth, I willed myself to stop.

I was less afraid than I had been that first time, but still scared enough to be ambivalent. I wanted to step on the gas and lose him, but I also wanted to roust him out of his ugly car and see his damned face. At the very least, I wanted to get a better look at the car and another look at the size and gait of this person, however disguised.

The car—the Pontiac name, missing its *o*, was written in chrome across the front—lurched to a halt, just touching my bumper. But the driver didn't get out, didn't wave a righteous fist, didn't shout obscenities. His face was barely visible and looked distorted—by a pantyhose mask? I couldn't tell. He backed up a few inches and came forward again, nudging.

I sat there, a challenge set in immobility, thinking as fast as I could. If I raced ahead, veered suddenly into a driveway, shot back out again behind him, maybe he would come out of the car. Of course, I'd be in the same rotten position I'd been in a couple of nights before—blocked from moving forward, forced into a reverse escape. Or worse yet, boxed into a driveway. Why the hell don't these damned Bay Area cities have alleys, I wondered, like any self-respecting town in the Midwest? I could only go forward or backward. There was no sideways.

I don't know what made me think I could sit like an idiot and wait for him to act first. Maybe it was because he hadn't shot at me the first time we'd met.

This time, he did.

My dashboard exploded, just to the right of the steering wheel.

Forward now seemed like a good idea. I stepped down hard on the gas and donated some Michelin rubber to the city of Berkeley. The brown Pontiac stayed right behind me all the way to MLK. When I turned left, the Pontiac turned right.

I drove another half-mile, keeping a steady check on my rear. No sign of the brown Pontiac. But my right arm was burning, and felt wet. Thinking the bullet must have grazed me, I pulled over and parked to check out the damage.

A two-inch chunk of dashboard plastic was sticking out of my forearm. The bile rose into my throat; I swallowed it, gripped the plastic, and yanked.

Not too bad. One brief cry, a few tears down the cheeks, but the damage looked minimal. The gash was ugly, more than an inch long and thick as the plastic, but didn't look very deep. Stitches might be advisable, but the bleeding didn't seem excessive. Sitting for two hours in some depressing hospital waiting room full of sick and bloody people—*that* seemed excessive. I decided to skip the emergency room. Rummaging in the dash compartment I found, underneath a flashlight and jammed behind a pile of maps, a blue silk scarf I had once liked. I wrapped it around my arm.

The damage to the car wasn't crippling, either. The rear window was a mess, with a clear bullethole in the middle of the spiderweb of cracked glass. The dashboard had some pieces missing, but they weren't vital organs. I drove the rest of the way to Lorene's.

Willie and Nathan were standing on the sidewalk next door to Lorene's house when I pulled up. As I approached her steps I glanced at them; they both looked away. Maybe it was because I'd dumped Nathan off the hood of my car the last time we'd met, or maybe the sight of my weird pursuer or my fast and nearly homicidal reverse course down the street that night had scared them.

Or, possibly, their manners could be attributed to the blood dripping down my arm, tonight, from underneath a blue silk scarf.

Lorene was home. She looked surprised to see me, and not at all happy.

I walked in the door past her. She closed it behind me, but stood near it, willing me to go.

A voice called from upstairs, "Who is it, Lorene?"

"It's okay, grandma! It's my teacher again!" Aside, to me, "Her ankles are all swollen. She doesn't do the stairs too good. What's wrong with your—"

"Be sure and offer her some coffee!"

"Okay!" Lorene was trying to get a look at my arm. "Want some coffee?"

"No. Thanks."

"What happened? You look real pissed off— excuse me, but you do."

"I always look this way when someone's been shooting me." I waved my arm in her face. Melodramatic, but what the hell, she was just a kid.

My words had the desired effect.

"Oh, lord—how bad is it? Is the bullet still in there? Sit down, please. Or do you want to go to the hospital?"

Her concern and alarm looked real enough, but

I didn't sit. I sneered at her suggestion of the hospital.

"Why didn't you tell me Jane was having an affair with Anderson?"

She sighed heavily and flopped down in a large armchair.

"I can't take much more of this," she said.

"Neither can I."

"Okay, she was having an affair with Anderson. But it was already over." Lorene glared at me defiantly. "She didn't kill the creep. She broke it off, and she didn't like him so much anymore."

"When? When did she break it off?"

"A couple of weeks before he got himself killed."

"Why?"

"She found out his wife had been sick the whole time, real sick. It made her mad."

"And how did she find that out?"

"I think your arm is still bleeding. Is there a bullet in it? Can I look at it? Can I bandage it for you?"

Let her suffer whatever guilt she's entitled to, I thought. Let her think I'm standing here, unmoved and unflinching, with a bullet in my arm.

"How did she find out?"

"Mr. Harwood told her."

"Did Mr. Harwood know she was seeing Anderson?"

"He never said so, not that I know of anyway. It just came up, you know, casually, that Mrs. Anderson was sick. I think."

"Did Jane know that Harwood and Ms. Anderson were close friends?"

"I think she saw them together once—yes, I remember her wondering about them. Do you mean, like *really* close friends?"

"I don't know. How long did Jane's affair with Anderson last?"

"About a month I think. Maybe two."

"She was still seeing Mark during that time?"

"Yes. Most of the time."

"Did he know what was going on?"

"Not that I know of. They were having more fights and stuff, but she never said he knew. And he never told me he knew. Course I'm not all that close to him." Maybe you are, I thought, now that Jane's gone.

"What about Rob Harwood? Did Jane have an affair with him?"

"She kinda liked him. But if she started anything with him she didn't say so."

"What do you think about him?"

She shrugged. "Nervous. Conceited. But maybe okay. He pushed at Jane sometimes to work harder and do more. I think she liked that."

"Where's Jane, Lorene?"

She shook her head.

"Why did she run?"

She shrugged. "You really should let me look at your arm. I'm a good nurse."

I ignored her offer again. I didn't want to break the flow of our conversation.

"How did she react when Anderson was killed?"

"She was real upset. For more than a week she couldn't talk about it at all. Then, right before she went away . . ." I waited, afraid to breathe lest I interrupt her, make her think better about telling me something, any little thing. "She said she just couldn't stand it, it was all really awful. Because it was all her fault that he got killed."

"What did she mean by that?"

"I don't know, she wouldn't say. But if it was her fault, I don't want to help her get in trouble." Lorene started to cry. "I have to go get a tissue."

"Wait a minute!" I dug desperately through all my pockets and came up with a tissue that was nearly clean. She took it and blew her nose.

"Did Mark know she said that, about it being her fault?"

"I told him, after she left. It freaked him out."

"How did it freak him out?"

"I guess he thought she was confessing something. But she didn't do it!"

"Who did?"

"I don't know."

"Is she afraid that whoever killed Anderson will kill her, too?"

"She never said, but I'm scared half to death for her now—look at your arm. It's still bleeding."

I weakened and looked at it. I didn't see any new blood.

"Did she tell you she was going to run away?"

Lorene hesitated. "Yeah. She said she was going. But I'm not telling anybody where she went, because I don't know!"

She refused to say another word about Jane and

insisted, once again, on looking at my arm. This time I let her look. She untied the silk scarf.

"It's a cut," she said, "not a bullet wound at all." She sounded disappointed.

"Shrapnel," I said. "The bullet hit my dash. I pulled a piece of plastic out."

She clucked, shaking her head. "You should have stitches, maybe."

"It's not that bad. It's not even bleeding anymore."

She *tsk*-ed and left the room, returning with some swabs, a bottle of peroxide, and a box of bandages. She cleaned the cut and put four little adhesive butterflies across it.

By the time she had finished it was eight-thirty, and Charlie was due at nine. She wasn't going to talk anymore, and I was ready for some R & R.

I half expected to find Nathan sitting on my car—I still hadn't gotten that headlight fixed—and a brown Pontiac double-parked beside me, but my departure from Lorene's neighborhood was peaceful and in first, second, and third gears.

The doorbell rang when I was still in the shower. Since I don't have such a thing as a good robe, and since so far Charlie and I had done little more than suggest an eventful second date, I kept him waiting outside while I put on a fresh shirt and my best jeans. I let him see my bare feet, bare face, and wet hair, lucky him.

I handed him a bottle of wine and a corkscrew and pointed him in the direction of the wineglasses.

"I'll just go dry my hair. Won't be a minute."

"Good." He smiled, and for the second time that evening my stomach dropped—a drop with a different quality than the shot-at kind of drop. Charlie has dark brown hair, heavy brows over brooding hazel eyes, cheekbones to die for, and a mouth that, honest to God, looks just like Brando's.

After I'd finished getting ready, we settled in with a glass of wine and discussed dinner. Then we had another glass of wine and couple of kisses. He got me talking about what I'd been doing that week, and bless his heart, admired my bandaged arm and expressed astonishment, admiration, and fear for my safety.

"I know you can take care of yourself, Barrett," he said. "But you must be ready for some heavy relaxation. Comfort food, that's what you need. Chicken soup, maybe."

"You're Italian, Charlie. What do you know about chicken soup?"

"Everything."

We kissed a few more times, talked about the case some more. I tried to get him to talk about his week, but he laughed at me.

"Landscape architecture is not the most exciting thing we can talk about," he said.

I marveled again at how advanced he was for his thirty-one years of life.

Somewhere between talk of sushi and masked bandits, we gave up on the idea of dinner altogether.

We went out for breakfast around one A.M., then went back to my place and back to bed.

22

Thursday. The last day of school, a half-day with no classes. The ones who showed up came to say good-bye. Mark didn't bother. Lorene stopped by to see how I was. I couldn't find Rob.

How was I? Tired. My arm was okay, but I hadn't gotten much sleep the night before and I'd been running on snacks and vitamins and excitement and anger for days. I made a couple of phone calls, one to Floyd Borden and one to my doctor's office. Yes, Borden said, Thursday night was one of Jane's regular nights. And Mark's, too. Sure, come on by and show him some pictures, he'd be delighted. I left several questions with my doctor's nurse, who promised she'd leave the answers on my phone machine within a couple of hours.

At noon I went to a quiet, elegant restaurant for a quiet, elegant, solitary lunch, no wine.

After lunch, I called my home phone to get my messages. Tito had gone to Santa Rosa again. My doctor said that a woman who'd had a bilateral mastectomy in September would probably be capable of stabbing someone to death by April, but if she'd just finished a course of chemotherapy she would be pretty worn out.

"All in all, Barrett," she said, "I would say she'd have to be pretty damned mad at someone to summon the strength. Now do me a favor. Call me back and let me know why in the name of God you're asking me this question."

I would, just as soon as I had the answer.

Full of expensive food, relaxed and mellowed by expensive ambiance, I went to see—it felt almost sacrilegious—Floyd Borden.

He was only too happy to see me.

"Well, there she is, my favorite private eye!"

"And you're my favorite supermarket manager," I said, deadpan, as I slid into the little plastic chair once more.

"This is pleasant, all right," he said, nodding and grinning. "What can I do for you?"

"Do you have a good memory for faces, Mr. Borden?"

"What do I have to do to get you to call me Floyd?"

"I'll call you whatever you want, Floyd," I answered evenly.

"How about 'sweetheart'? You know, 'Let Me Call You Sweetheart.' "

For once he correctly read my expression—it was murderous—and backed down.

"Oh, come now, just kidding. Faces? I've got a great memory for faces."

I knew he would say that. Whether it was true or not remained to be seen. I opened the yearbook to the photos of The Mummers Club and pointed to the mug shot of Rob Harwood.

"What about this face? Do you recall seeing it before?"

He studied the picture, then pointed to a group shot where Harwood was directing. "Same guy here, right?"

Terrific, I thought. He can identify a picture in the yearbook from a picture in the yearbook. "Yes. Same guy. What I want to know is, have you ever seen him here, in the store? Does his face look at all familiar to you?"

Someone knocked on the door and he called out. "Yeah! Come in!" It was one of the courtesy clerks I'd seen around the store.

"You wanted to see me?" She looked like she hoped it wasn't true.

"Yeah. I hope you can help out," he said to her. "Somebody's got to work Mark's hours for the next couple of days. You interested in some extra time?"

She told him she was, and she could fill in.

"What's that all about?" I asked.

"You mean about Mark? Darned kids—he tells me today he's got to take a couple of days off; family problems, he says."

"Is he working his regular hours today?"

"Just till seven tonight. He even insisted on getting off early! He's a helluva fine employee, but a little more notice would have been nice." He turned his attention back to the yearbook and studied the picture of Harwood some more. "You know how it is, you live in this area, you see people every day, on the street . . . but yes. He definitely looks familiar. I've seen him before. Kind of a handsome, faggoty little guy.'' He inflated his own chest as he spoke.

"He's a friend of mine,'' I snarled. A dumb thing to say under the circumstances, but I couldn't help myself. I hate that super-hetero crap.

"Oh, no offense or anything, that's just how he struck me.''

"So he looks familiar—have you seen him here, in the store?'' Rob had said he shopped at the SaveMor, but that's not all I was after.

"Yes. Absolutely.''

"Do you remember seeing him here the night Anderson was killed?''

He looked at the photo with greater interest. "You think he did it? Your friend?''

"I have no idea. Was he here that night?''

Borden sighed. "You know, doll, I'd sure like to help you out, but I just don't remember for sure. I just can't say yes and I can't say no. Hey!'' he said suddenly, pointing to the picture where Jane hovered in the background. "That's Jane, right? That reminds me—yeah, that's why I remember his face. I saw her talking to him once or twice.''

"At length?''

"No. I'd remember that. There's too much work to do around here. . . . ''

"You saw Jane talking to Anderson, too, isn't that right?''

"Sure. He was a real regular.''

"How did they act together? Jane and this man? Did you ever see anything unusual, anything more than just hello and a little small talk?"

He thought, cast me a sly glance. "If they did more than that, they didn't do it in front of me."

"So you never saw anything but friendly small talk between Jane and Anderson and between Jane and Harwood?"

"That's all I saw."

"Jane's stepfather stopped in to see her once in a while, too. Did you ever meet him?"

"You know, I didn't exactly meet him, but I had some words with Jane about him, and that was when she told me he was her stepfather."

"Words?"

"You bet. It was her body English or something, her attitude. And her tone of voice sounded snotty. I didn't hear what she said to him, but I thought she was mouthing off to a customer. When I went over to put a stop to it she introduced us. Seemed like a nice guy. Sharp, friendly. Kids! They don't know when they're well off."

"When was that?"

He thought for a while, pulling at his lower lip with his index finger.

"I don't know. A while ago. Couple months, maybe."

"Do you remember seeing him after that, like around the time Anderson died or the week Jane disappeared?"

"Sorry, I don't."

I took the snapshot of Elizabeth and William Anderson out of my bag.

"Have you ever seen this woman?"

He gazed at the picture.

"Not a very good photograph. Hard to say. Who's the guy with her?"

So much for his memory for faces.

"William Anderson."

"Not a good photograph at all. I can tell you one thing, though—she wasn't the one who ran out of here screaming the night he was killed. That one was little and dark."

That's big news, I thought. Everyone who knew there'd been a killing knew that.

Nothing. His memory remained unjogged.

I opened the yearbook again, and turned to the pages of graduating seniors, found the P's, and showed him Purvis's photo.

"What about him?"

"Friend of Jane's, huh?"

"I don't know."

"I don't either." He shook his head. "I can't help you here. Maybe yes, maybe no."

"One more thing."

"You can have as many things as you want."

I ignored the comment. "I'd like to show your employees these photos, too—anyone who might have been here the night of the murder, especially."

"Okay, let me set that up."

"And I didn't look at the produce room the last time I was here. I'd like to see it."

"How about you sit back there and I run people through to you?"

"Terrific. Do me one more favor—send Mark Hanlon in last."

The produce room was full of crates of produce, logically enough. It smelled damp and fruity. The room had a regular door—the one that had been unlocked the night of the murder—and a loading dock bay. Both were open today. A man was unloading crates of oranges, dollying them in from the back of a truck pulled up to the dock.

Borden brought in two chairs and kept a steady stream of checkers and courtesy clerks moving into the room and out again. I understood at last what Tito had meant about the "boring parts." A number of the courtesy clerks were tech students and recognized both Anderson and Harwood. A few thought they recognized Elizabeth Anderson, but could come up with nothing concrete.

I checked names off against my list of people who had been there the night of the murder. Only a couple of those were absent.

Finally, Mark appeared. He was moving slowly. His eyes were red and tired-looking. He sat.

"You want to show me some pictures, Ms. Lake? That's what everybody says—pictures. Who of?"

"This woman." I showed him the photo of the Andersons. He looked at it, frowned, shook his head. "That's Anderson. Is that his wife or something?"

"Yes."

"Never saw her."

"Borden tells me you've got family problems, Mark. What's up?"

He stared at me. "Jesus. I can't believe this. He had no right to tell you anything."

I had a moment's pleasant image of Mark punching Borden in the face, but decided to tell the truth anyway.

"He didn't exactly tell me. I was in his office when it came up—he was looking for someone to replace you."

"Well, there's nothing wrong. I lied to him. This was the last day of school. I wanted a couple of days to just hang out, maybe go to the beach. I'm tired. I never take any time off. Is that okay with you?"

"Sure. Have a nice time. You deserve a rest. But tell me something—did you call Mr. Broz's office and say that Jane was in LA?"

He hesitated for only a moment. "Yeah. I did."

"Why?"

"Because that's where I thought she was. That's where she told me she was going. The day before she left. She told me at work. I was pretty upset."

I remembered Borden saying the two had had an intense conversation. I also remembered that Mark had denied it when I'd asked him about it the first time.

"But she's not there."

He shrugged. "That's where she told me she was going. But I guess not."

"Why did you tip us off?"

"I was worried about her, I guess. I don't know."

"Do you know where she really is?"

"No. I don't."

"Does Lorene?"

"I wouldn't know that."

"I think she does. And I think she wouldn't tell me because she thought Jane might be in trouble. If you thought telling where she was—where you thought she was—might get her in trouble, why did you do it?"

"It seemed like maybe she could get help or something." He wasn't convincing me.

"Maybe you were—just for a few days—angry with her and wanted her found?"

He was looking at his hands. Big, strong hands. "What would I be angry about? No. That wasn't it."

"Weren't you angry because you knew about her and Anderson?"

He flushed red, the color starting at the open neck of his shirt and moving like a wave up to the top of his face. He didn't answer me.

"What about Rob Harwood—did you know about him, too?"

His head shot up, his bloodshot eyes meeting mine.

"Harwood! I never heard anything about that. No! That's not true."

Maybe it wasn't. "But you did find out about Anderson."

He dropped his head again. I waited. He didn't say anything.

"Did Lorene tell you?"

"Yeah."

"When did she tell you?"

His gaze drifted around the room, as if he were

trying to collect information from it. Then, instead, he seemed to collect himself. He sat up straighter.

"After Jane left."

"Not before he got killed?"

His face turned even redder. "After Jane left!" he spat at me.

"What did you think when Lorene told you that Jane blamed herself for Anderson's murder?"

He rubbed his eyes, grimaced, stood, and moved closer to the door. He spoke wearily. "She never said that. That's crazy. I'm going back to work now."

He walked out of the room. I sat there for a few minutes, thinking about him.

When, I wondered, had Mark really found out about Jane and Anderson? He must have noticed Anderson's regular visits to the market. How hard would it have been for him to kill Anderson, run through this room, stash his bloody clothing somewhere nearby, change, and return to the body along with the others, in time to identify it for Borden? According to Tito's notes, the police had searched the cars in the lot, the dumpster, and the hill above the market, and found nothing. But Mark probably knew the store and the area around it well. Better than the cops did.

There was no law that said nice young men, quiet young men, couldn't commit crimes of passion. It all depended, I supposed, on why they were nice and quiet.

23

Harwood's condo complex was a small, neat one, with tall trees and short-cropped green lawns that must be hard to keep alive during these water-rationing drought years. Rob Harwood's attached house was at the back, away from the street, shaded and quiet. His car was in the carport with his number on it.

He came to the door wearing a pair of neat faded jeans and an incredibly white T-shirt. He frowned when he saw that I was the one who had come to call, but invited me in. Seeing his place—the furniture was sparse, glass and steel and leather, with no litter on the surfaces—I reflected that possibly he'd been hoping for someone tidier. Detective work was hell on the wardrobe. My skirt was wrinkled, I'd snagged my pantyhose on a crate in the produce room, and my shirt smelled like rotten vegetation.

"What's up, Barrett?" He waved me in, still frowning.

"I wanted to talk more to you about Jane. I feel that I've still got too many unanswered questions about her."

"I answered all your questions!" he snapped. Then, as an afterthought, "Well, I'm kind of tired, but sit down for a while."

"I wonder if I could have a glass of water. I'm really thirsty."

He shrugged and disappeared into the kitchen, returning with two bottles of Evian water and two glasses with ice. Even though he was annoyed by my unannounced appearance at his door, he couldn't bring himself to serve tap water. I kind of like tap water.

"So, why are you here again, really? Has someone been telling you stories?"

"No stories, Rob. Did you know Jane was having an affair with William Anderson?"

He stared at me. "No, I did not. Why would I know something like that?"

"If you didn't know, why did you tell Jane that Anderson's wife was sick? You don't seem to have told anyone else."

"Let's see," he murmured, sipping at his glass of water. "I'm trying to remember how that came about . . . Yes, that's right. It was because of that night at the theater."

I waited patiently while he got his story together.

"Elizabeth and I had gone to the Berkeley Rep. At intermission, we ran into Jane. She was with that boy, Mark. I introduced them, we chatted about the play. The next week Jane asked me about Elizabeth—did we go to plays together a lot, that sort of thing. She remarked that she'd thought Elizabeth hadn't looked very well. At the time Elizabeth was still on her chemo, wearing a scarf to hide what was left of her hair—she did look pretty sick. It was toward the end of the treatment. So I told Jane what was wrong.

"Come to think of it, I did think Jane reacted pretty strongly to the news, since she'd just met the woman. But Jane could be like that. Emotional. Lots of empathy."

The phone rang in another room and he got up to answer it. I heard a few words here and there. He was telling someone that the tenant would be waiting to let him in. Something about fixing a sink. He told him to send the bill to the condo address. Income property on a teacher's pay? He must have inherited the money. Or maybe he was just smarter than I am.

When he came back I asked him if he was shocked to hear about the affair.

"Of course I am. I'm shocked and surprised." Was he? Hard to tell. Acting was his business, after all.

"Really? Why would you be surprised? You say Jane flirted with you. Don't you think she would have followed through if you'd been willing?"

"I'm not shocked so much about Jane as I am about Anderson. I just wouldn't have thought it of him, I guess."

"How did you feel when Jane came on to you, Rob? How did you handle it?"

"Well, let me think." While he was thinking I got up and wandered over to his bookcase.

He had a small section of erotica that included the Marquis de Sade, and both a paperback and hardcover edition of *Lolita*. I pulled down the hardcover. It was an autographed copy.

Feeling a little too much like Jesse Helms, I sat down again.

"She's an attractive young woman," Harwood began. "I guess I can understand why someone who was not strong enough would, well, succumb. But I just put it out of my mind."

"Did you ever talk to her about it?"

"No. I just never encouraged her."

"Where were you the night Anderson was killed?"

He smiled sardonically. "I can't believe you actually said that."

I shrugged, and couldn't help smiling back.

"I don't know how else it could be said."

"What was the date?"

"April eighth. It was a Thursday night."

He got up and went to a desk at the far end of the room, pulled a book out of the drawer.

"I was at a political meeting. Council candidate."

"Can I see that?"

"Of course not! You don't have a search warrant. You can't just expect me to hand over my private possessions."

"Please?"

He shook his head in disbelief and handed it over. The entry said "Meeting, 8:30" and the name of the council candidate. I did notice that it was written in black ink, while all the other entries for that week were in blue.

"How many people were at that meeting?"

"Couple dozen, maybe. Listen . . ."

"Any names you can give me?"

"No. I don't remember who was there, and I didn't go with anyone. And I've had enough of this. Really, Barrett, you've gone power-mad." He stood. I got up, too. I was almost finished with him for now. There were things I needed to do before I talked to him again.

"Could be, Rob. One more question . . ."

He glared at me, cold eyes in a face carved of rock.

"You said The Mummers Club holds its meetings on Mondays. Did Jane attend the first meeting after Spring Break?"

"Sure. Jane attended all the meetings."

"But that was her last one."

"That's right. It was her last one. And that was your last question."

"Only for now, Rob."

Outside, I looked at my watch and hurried to the Mazda. It was 4:30. The day was getting away from me. The car lots would be closing soon, and I wanted to take one more look at the merchandise at Empire Used Autos.

I got there in twenty minutes.

A different salesman, someone I hadn't seen on my first visit, approached me. He had dark, slicked-back hair and he was wearing much too much aftershave. He smelled like a blown rose.

I told him I was just looking. He hovered while I searched the lot. The car that looked so much like the one driven by my masked friend that first night at Lorene's was still there. And just a few feet away was the brown Pontiac from the night before, the one with the *o* missing from the hood. I could still see minute traces of black muck on one edge of the front license plate. The license number included a two and an A. Just looking at the car made the bandaged gash on my arm ache.

"How long has this car been on the lot?" I asked the salesman.

"A week or two. Why?"

I thought about how to phrase the next question.

"I guess it is the same one, then. I went to look at it when the owner was selling it on his own. He said if I didn't buy it he was going to trade it in, that was why he was offering such a good deal. You're asking a lot more than he was." I peered in the window. "Gee, I think it's got more miles on it now, too. He wasn't driving it. Do you guys drive these cars often?"

He looked defensive. "No. Hardly at all. Maybe it's just mileage from test drives."

"A hundred miles?"

"You must remember it wrong."

I didn't remember it at all, of course. I'd never seen the inside of this car before.

"But people connected with this lot—the owner, the salespeople—have access to the cars, right? Couldn't someone have put that many miles on it?"

"Look, I can get the price down a little, if that's what you want, but I really doubt that anyone here drove this old car that many miles. Maybe someone borrowed it for an hour or something, but—''

''One of the salespeople?''

''Well, maybe Billy did. I didn't.''

''Billy? Is he the salesman who was working yesterday?''

''Yeah. It's just me and him. But they don't encourage us sales guys to take the cars, you know? You say you were here yesterday?'' He was beginning to get that look, that ''What's with this nut?'' look, but he wasn't as bright or as suspicious as Billy.

''Or of course, one of the owners could have.''

''Yeah. One of them could have—look, this car's as good as it was when you saw it before. Now, suppose you tell me what the private party was asking for it. . . .''

I told him I wasn't sure I wanted it, but if he could cut the price in half I'd go home and think about it.

''I'd have to get an okay to go down that far, and I'm the only one here. But I can make a phone call.''

''You do that,'' I told him. ''And I'll come back tomorrow.''

''Listen, how about I take three hundred off right now, and . . .''

His voice faded as I walked away.

Someone was borrowing cars from this lot to chase me with. I'd met both the salesmen, and as far as I knew neither one of them was connected with the case. One of them could have been a hired gun, but I doubted it. I'd also met one

owner, Jack Calderini, but I knew now that someone else probably had a share in his place, because today's salesman had confirmed my offhand
reference to "one of the owners." Once again, I
looked at my watch. Too late to check business
licenses at City Hall.

I made a couple of phone calls. One to Neil Clapton's office—no one answered—and one to Lorene.

Lorene said she didn't remember for sure
whether Jane had seen Mark during Spring Break,
since they'd been arguing off and on. She didn't
think so.

I drove back to North Berkeley and hung around
outside Harwood's condo for a while. His car was
still there, and he didn't come out. Then I went
to Elizabeth Anderson's house. As I watched, she
stepped out the door, watered a couple of ferns
hanging on the porch, and stepped back inside. I
made a mental note of the description and make
of the car parked in her driveway.

Some night, I thought, if my pantyhosed pal
shows up again, I may want to drive over to Empire Used Autos and see if the everyday transportation of someone I know is parked there—the
car owned by someone who had driven there to
get a nighttime loaner.

I wasn't sure who that person would be, but I
had some very strong suspicions that I thought
would soon be proved correct.

First, I wanted to see if I could find out how
Mark Hanlon was going to spend his days off.

He had been planning, according to Borden, to

leave work by seven that night. I got to his street at 6:45.

Once again, I drove around the corner and watched his front door.

He pulled up at 7:15 and ran into the house, emerging in a few minutes with a backpack in his hand. He was still moving fast, and tripped at the curb just as he reached his car. The pack swung into his fender.

I was fifty feet away, but when that pack hit the car it hit hard, with the sound of heavy metal hitting metal.

24

Mark yanked open his car door, tossed his pack into the backseat, started the still-warm car, and took off, with me not too far behind him.

I followed him down Ashby to the freeway. At first I thought he might be going to San Francisco, but he cut onto 880 at the interchange and kept on going south.

He was driving ten miles over the limit. Less than an hour later, more than halfway to San Jose, he signaled for an exit at Mountain View.

Half a mile down the road he pulled into a shopping center, parked in front of a diner, and went inside. I parked out of sight, near a pay phone.

Maybe this was our destination, maybe not. I might not know where I was going, but I wanted someone to know I was going there, and where I'd stopped along the way. I punched Gilda's number. I knew she'd probably be home on a Thursday night.

"You said you wanted to help me with his case, right?"

"Where are you?"

"Mountain View. Following Jane's boyfriend, Mark. For all I know I'm going to LA. I don't know where Tito is or when he'd get a message, and I may not have time for more than one phone call, so I want you to do two things for me."

"Anything!" She sounded thrilled.

"First, call our office phone"—I gave her the number, even though I thought she had it—"and leave a message telling Tito what's happening— where I am now and that I'm on the road, maybe to Jane. Second, first thing tomorrow, go down to Oakland City Hall and check the business tax records for Empire Used Autos on Broadway. I want to know the names of the owners."

"Got it. Good luck."

I blessed her in my heart for not telling me to be careful, climbed back into my car, and waited for Mark to reappear.

I had a not-quite-full tank of gas. Mark's car would go farther without refueling than mine would. If he was, indeed, going all the way to LA I had a problem. I'd have to stop, and I'd lose him.

Mark was out of the diner in ten minutes, carrying a bag. He got back in his car and turned again toward the freeway.

It wasn't long before I realized that a trip all the way south was unlikely. Mark was obviously in a hurry. He hadn't taken the time to eat at the diner, but had grabbed some takeout. And yet he was staying on 880. If he'd been bound for LA he'd have cut over east, to Route 5, a fast, direct,

not very pretty way to go, or even to the slower
101.

We were heading for the coast. No one who
isn't sightseeing takes Highway 1 to LA.

We could be on our way to Monterey or Carmel. Great vacation spots. Maybe he *was* just taking a couple of days off. At any rate, the RX7
would make it as far as Carmel without more gas.

When we reached the ocean he exited at Santa
Cruz and drove to the big municipal lot at the
edge of the Santa Cruz Beach Boardwalk, the last
great Edwardian seaside amusement park on the
West Coast, the one the moviemakers used for
that wonderful flick, *Lost Boys*. A playground for
boy vampires, and Mark Hanlon's apparent destination—unless this was just another pit stop.

He parked at the quiet outer edge of the lot,
although there were plenty of spaces closer in. I
parked two rows over and several cars down from
his, got out, and followed his footsteps through
drifting fog toward the bright, haloed lights and
spinning, looney-tunes hysteria of the Boardwalk.
Mark's pack was slung heavily over his shoulder.

It was prime time, 8:30 in the evening, just getting dark. The sparse crowd was bundled up
against the chilled, damp air. The thin fog softened the gaudy carny edge, dreamlike. Screams
from the Giant Dipper and the Rock-O-Plane
punctuated the background lilt of the calliope and
the hum of talk and laughter. The smells of salt
water, cotton candy, and hot dogs permeated everything, including the skin and clothing of people who brushed by me. A balloon vendor dressed

as a clown strolled by on stilts, cackling and scaring little children, hideously reminiscent of Pennywise in Stephen King's *It*. He was walking in the right direction, so I used him for cover as I trailed Mark past ice cream sandwiches, past ringtosses, past short lines of hyped-up kids and grinning grownups.

My thin jacket was not quite warm enough.

The giant pirate ship was rocking back and forth in its made-for-amusement storm, kids and adults screeching with joy and fear as it tilted up high, nearly standing on its prow. Mark got in line at a ticket booth nearby.

The young woman selling tickets was Jane Wahlman. I had done it. I had actually found her. I wasn't sure what to do next, though, so I decided to stay hidden and observe.

Pennywise the balloon vendor kept on strolling, so I slid out from behind him and sidled up on an ice cream stand with a view of the ticket booth. Jane was shaking her head. Mark was waving his arms, pointing back toward the car lot. She looked at her watch and said something to him. He argued some more, then shook his head and posted himself, sentryike, beside her booth.

Half an hour later, someone else showed up to manage the booth and Jane and Mark began to walk back toward the lot.

I walked behind them, as closely as I dared. The music was loud, the people boisterous. The only piece of their exchange I heard was when she shouted "I can't tell . . . Mother!" and Mark yelled back ". . . kill you, too!"

Then they got quieter again.

Through the parking lot, I stayed out of sight by creeping along behind cars. The lot was dark after the glare of the strip, the fog was getting thicker, and I had no trouble keeping barriers between me and them. We passed through the more congested area, with its foot and car traffic, and into the quiet and dimness of the lot's hinterland. I stopped at my car and watched Mark and Jane continue on to his.

Mark glanced around nervously, shifting his pack from his shoulder to his hand.

They got in his car, but he didn't start it. Carefully, soundlessly, I opened my hatch and pulled out my tire iron. Easing the hatch closed again, I crouched down and skittered along the side of my car, preparing to sneak closer, wondering whether to try to listen to their conversation or simply rap on the window, wave my tire iron, and demand that Mark drop his gun or crowbar or whatever it was he was carrying and that Jane come home and come clean. I was tensely aware that if Mark did have a gun, I was ill-prepared to make any demands.

As I hesitated, glancing down the row of cars for a way to get closer invisibly, I saw an old car parked in a no-parking area that was part of the outer lane. No one was in the driver's seat. Just another anonymous-looking car with a couple of dents, a faded paint job. Forgettable. Except that I'd done a careful reconnaissance of Empire Auto that afternoon, and this could very well be the gray Ford I'd seen there. A moment later I was thanking whatever instinct had kept me from breaking cover and bulling my way over to Mark and Jane, because I caught a glimpse, through the windows, of someone's bobbing head on the other side of the Ford.

The figure moved forward toward the front of the car, toward a better angle of vision on Mark's Datsun.

I didn't know, absolutely know, that the two young people were in danger. I didn't absolutely know that this person had followed me following Mark to Santa Cruz, was a killer, had a weapon, and was going to use it.

What I did know was that if all of this was so, my tire iron wouldn't cut it, and I had only one real weapon of my own. I unlocked and started my car. No movement from behind the Ford. I backed out slowly and drove toward it. As I passed along its large rear end, I saw someone scurry around its front.

I stepped on the gas and swung hard around the Ford, grazing its bumper.

Neil Clapton stopped at a Volkswagen parked at the end of Mark's row, hunched down to shelter beside its front left fender, and aimed a large gun at me while I aimed my car at him. He got off a couple of rounds before I rammed the RX7 into the Volkswagen, my low, sharp front end pinning his legs between clamps of dented metal.

He screamed. I've never heard another creature scream that way before. I've never been in a war or a bad accident or a slaughterhouse or a hunting preserve or a research laboratory. He was waving his arms, and I didn't see the gun in his hands anymore. I got out of my car, dazed by the impact. Clapton was still screaming. Mark and Jane were running toward me, Mark with a gun in his moronic adolescent hand. So were about a half dozen other people, while another dozen or so ran the other way.

"Damn it, Mark!" I yelled. "Put the gun away!" I was willing to bet he didn't have a permit. He stuck it down his pants.

Clapton stopped screaming. He'd passed out.

I stared at him, not able to focus on the people gathering around me. I shook off—with Mark's help—a middle-aged man who tried to grab my arms, thinking, probably, that he was detaining a homicidal maniac.

Then I climbed back in my car and backed up a couple of feet. Clapton dropped to the ground. I turned off the engine. As I sat there feeling victorious, sated, exhausted, and nauseated, I told myself to be sure to leave a note on the Volkswagen's windshield. Then I noticed that my own windshield, on the passenger side, had been shattered by one of Clapton's bullets.

25

Two days after I'd broken both of Neil Clapton's legs and the police had carted him back to Berkeley, Floyd Borden put a cap on the case against Clapton by catching the screaming woman.

He'd spotted the small, dark-haired witness walking out the door with a large package of steaks, only half-hidden under her coat. She confessed that on the night of the murder, she had seen the bloodied killer running away from his victim. Panicked and horrified, she'd been unable to keep herself from screaming and running—screaming at the sight of the crime, and running because she'd called attention to herself and her pockets were full of butter and meat and canned beans.

As a career thief, she'd had no interest in coming forward later and helping the police. But Borden promised not to press shoplifting charges if she would testify now, and she agreed.

Of course, the case against Clapton was already pretty good. Gilda had learned that our real estate man-about-town was, indeed, a part owner of Empire Used Autos. Jane would testify that he had told her he'd killed Anderson. I had a few things to say about being shot at.

Even the woman who worked in his office was willing to add a word or two to the indictment.

When we were all feeling a bit less stunned, I invited Jane, Mark, and Lorene to have breakfast with me at a diner that made the best omelets in Berkeley. Mark declined. He didn't ever plan, he said, to see Jane again.

I suspected he was also sick to death of me.

Jane was recovering nicely, although she still looked pale and much too weary for a kid her age. Lorene was cheerful as hell, happy that her friend hadn't really killed anyone and was safely back on her home ground.

But Jane told us she didn't plan to sink any roots in that home ground just yet. She was going to make up a couple of tests and get her diploma, spend a couple of days with her father—the biological one, our satisfied and relieved client—and go back to the Boardwalk.

"I like it there," she told us. "My boss agreed to overlook my giving him a phony Social Security number. It's a fun place to work."

"And it's not like real life," Lorene observed sardonically.

"That's exactly right," Jane said. She actually laughed, and I felt reasonably hopeful about her future. Reasonably.

She was very interested in how I'd worked the case.

I explained that I'd had a problem from the beginning with the timing of her disappearance, nearly two weeks after the murder. Once I'd learned that she'd been seeing Anderson—I put it as delicately as I could—I was sure that the one event was closely linked to the other and that she was involved in his death.

So why the lag time? Anderson was killed on the eighth. Why didn't she run until April 21? The most likely answer, I thought, was that it wasn't until the week of the 19th that she found out who the killer was, and felt threatened herself.

It would have been nice if I'd been able to take that theory and use it to narrow down the list of suspects: "Aha! This is the only person she didn't see during Spring Break!" But no such luck. There were too many on that list she could have been out of touch with: Mark, Rob Harwood—and, through Harwood, Elizabeth Anderson—as well as Jane's vacationing stepfather.

The fact that she'd seen one of my suspects, Rob, at The Mummers Club just two days before she took off had seemed pretty significant, but on the other hand there were a couple of stronger points that turned me toward Clapton.

First of all, Mark had told me that Jane had introduced him to her stepfather. She had told Mark that Clapton had "messed with her" when she was a child. Borden had seen her with Clapton and noticed her antagonistic behavior. Why, I wondered, would she introduce Mark to a man she despised?

I came up with a possibility: Maybe Clapton was still jealous of her, and possessive. Maybe she was tormenting him: "This is my boyfriend. Nyah

nyah nyah.'' Maybe she made a point of introducing him to her boyfriends.

And if she disliked the man so much, and if they never saw each other except when he stopped by the market, how did the woman in Clapton's office know that Jane was ''a lovely girl''?

I'd called her and asked her that, and it turned out that she'd met Jane only once—on Tuesday the 20th, when Jane had gone to see Clapton, desperate enough to actually seek him out, desperate to know if something she'd done had caused Anderson's death. What she had done was introduce Anderson to her stepfather, just as she'd introduced Mark, and taunted him with a lover close to his own age. A lover, she told him, who came to the store every Thursday night.

Clapton admitted he'd killed the man, and justified it to her by saying Anderson was an evil and sinful person. He boasted about the murder, and used a threat he'd often used effectively on her during all those years of abuse: If you tell, I'll kill your mother.

''Can you believe it?'' Jane asked sadly. ''It wasn't even jealousy so much, I think. There was guilt, too, and this weird moral indignation. He said he didn't plan it, that he just went back to the market that Thursday night to tell him to leave me alone. But when he saw him he wanted to kill him. So he did.''

After which, on his way out via the produce room, he'd dashed past a small shoplifter who was slipping a pound of butter down her blouse.

"And you thought it was your fault, so you ran away?" I asked.

"Mostly I ran because I was scared. Oh, I was afraid it was my fault before that. For a while I thought maybe Mark had done it, that he'd done it fast and gotten himself cleaned up somehow. But you know, he never really knew what was going on, not until after I'd gone, and Lorene told him about me and William."

"You lied to me about that," I told Lorene.

"I was embarrassed. Ashamed I'd told him a thing like that. I didn't want Jane ever to know I did—but, you know, with her taking off like that and saying it was her fault . . . I needed to tell someone."

"It's okay," Jane said. "Anyway, I never really thought Mark did it, not really, because I didn't think he loved me enough to do something that crazy."

But he was worried about her, as well as angry and terrified, as our investigation progressed, that he was a prime suspect, the one with the best motive for the murder. Finally, he managed to convince Lorene that Jane had to be found and brought back, for her own good—and his.

He'd taken the gun, a little snub-nosed job his mother had bought after a burglary, for self-protection, because Lorene had told him the killer had shot at me.

Clapton had admitted, soon after his arrest, that he'd never intended to keep that first appointment with me. He'd hidden in a doorway halfway down the block, watched me arrive and read his note. He wanted a good look at me, and my car. And he used what he saw to keep tabs on me and to try to scare me off the case. He'd been following me, and also Mark, because he hoped we'd lead him to Jane. Her disappearance had terrified him. She was out of his control, away from his threats, and he was afraid she might get strong enough to turn him in. He decided he'd be safer if she were dead.

When he followed me following Mark out of town, he was pretty sure we must be going to Jane. He had his pantyhose mask in the car with him, as always, that night, but he'd been so distraught about "having" to kill Jane he'd forgotten to put it on. They found it—the thing was a mass of runs by then, anyway—wrapped in the oversized raincoat in the backseat of the gray Ford.

"So you thought it was your stepfather, I mean, once you decided it wasn't Mark?" I asked. Jane was picking at her omelet and I was feeling guilty for ruining her appetite.

"Well, I thought of William's wife, too. I mean, can you imagine, with her being so sick—I feel really bad about that."

She had also suspected Rob Harwood, her favorite teacher, because she believed he was Elizabeth's lover. She was right about that. Now that the killer had been arrested and all but convicted, he and Elizabeth were being a lot less discreet about their relationship.

So no matter which way Jane looked, someone she cared about was involved and she was guilty of something. Responsible for Anderson's murder, for her mother's safety, for her stepfather's behavior—and still, after all these years, scared to death of the man.

Enough, I thought, of the past.

"So you're going back to Santa Cruz for a while. Then what?"

She picked up her fork and began to eat again.

"I don't know exactly. I was thinking about maybe going down to LA, going to acting school part-time—my dad says he'll help a little, financially." She smiled. "I guess this whole thing kind of got his attention."

"How about you, Lorene. College?"

"After I put together a little more money. I thought maybe next year I'd apply at UCLA."

Jane scooped up a forkful of home fries and shoveled them into her mouth. "She's afraid if she lets me go alone, she'll miss all the excitement."

"I'm afraid," Lorene said, pinching Jane's arm, "that if I let you go alone you'll excite yourself to death."

"Like Marilyn Monroe, she says." Jane shook her head.

Actually, I thought Jane looked more like Elizabeth Taylor.

"What about you, Ms. Lake?' Lorene asked. "You going to keep doing this detective gig?"

"Sure. If I can squeeze it in between piano lessons. By the way, would either of you be interested in adopting a kitten? Black-and-white, name of Franklin?"

They didn't think so. But I knew Rob Harwood was considering it.

After breakfast, I drove my new car—the Mazda was in the shop getting its headlight and its front end fixed, and I hadn't decided whether to sell it or not—over to the office to finish up some work with Tito and talk about the other cases that were coming in.

I'd paid just three thousand dollars for the car I was driving. I'd found it in the *East Bay Dealer*. Its colors were sedate—brown and cream. It was a four-door sedan. It needed a little work.

Tito was walking up to the office door as I parked in front. He stared at me as I got out, and looked at the car a long, long time.

"This is the new car?" he said. "The one you found in the paper? The Sedate Sedan?"

"Yes."

"You think a Mercedes 220S—what, a 1958?"

"Fifty-nine."

"You think that's inconspicuous?"

"It's brown. And it's got dual carburetors and a straight-six engine and it's fast and heavy."

"In case you have to run someone down."

I ignored that remark. "And the oak dashboard and window frames are nearly perfect."

The front end was perfect, too. I didn't want to use it as a weapon. Fortunately, in a few days I could go to the gun shop and pick up my .38.

"Okay, so take me for a ride in your work of art and I'll buy you a beer for a job well done. Maybe some dinner."

"I was hoping you'd say that—about the job well done."

We climbed into the car, I put it in first, and we began to roll down Telegraph.

"Because I've been thinking," I continued. About the kids who needed more than the educational system could ever give, than I could ever give working in the system. The ones who fell through the cracks. The Jane Wahlmans. Even the Pissed-off Purvises. About how much I liked catching bad guys. "Thinking I should give up teaching and sign on full-time as your apprentice."

"Not a chance."

"Why not?"

"You've been a teacher a long time. You like it more than you realize you do." He held up his hand to forestall my sputtering response. "And even if you don't, what if business goes down the toilet? I don't want to be responsible for you being on the street. With a shopping cart. Hang on to your day job, Barrett."

"Are you implying I'm not good enough?"

"You're terrific. A real talent. Maybe a little impetuous, but . . . what if you burn out on this? It's a tough business, a lot tougher than teaching. You could get depressed. You could get hurt. Things could dry up, no work."

I pulled up at the curb in front of The Elbow Room, switched off the ignition, and turned to face him.

"I don't need you to protect me, you paternalistic jerk! I'm over forty years old, and I've been without my daddy for more years than I like to think about.''

''I know you're not really mad,'' he said. ''You're just trying to scare me. It worked. I'm scared to death. Let's get that beer.''

''Not yet. I want to settle this.''

''Okay, here it is. I'm not protecting you. I'm protecting me—from guilt. I don't want to be responsible. I don't want to have to keep you on even if there's not enough business or it doesn't work out.''

''What if I find a way to do both: job-sharing, or part-time, or working night and day—something?''

''I don't want you to lose your pension and your tenure, or whatever the hell it is.''

''I'll stay nice and safe and you'll be off the hook. You can feel free to fire me any time you want.''

He grinned. ''I like the sound of that. Firing you any time I want.''

That was when I knew I had him.

**Be sure to catch
the next Barrett Lake mystery,
Picture of David, coming to you
from Signet in October 1993.**

I was on time, but the Minskys weren't ready for me. Lev was taking a nap, his wife explained, and she had been just about to wake him. She insisted I accept a cup of weak, scalding coffee, to keep me company until she returned to the living room.

She was back so quickly I hadn't gotten around to a second sip, and hadn't had a chance to do more than glance around the small apartment living room. She leaned against the back of the couch, across the coffee table from the overstuffed chair where I sat, her fingers gripping the fabric like a hawk lifting prey.

"I want to ask you," she said. "Are you sure you can help us find David?"

"I can't say. I need to know more about him and about what happened."

"He's fourteen. He's been kidnapped. What more do you need to know?"

"Why are you sure he was kidnapped? Do the police think so?"

"The police . . ." she shrugged with a sigh. "Can you help us?" She was pushing. I let myself be pushed.

"I'll try."

"Then I'll show you something. It came in the mail two days ago."

She walked rapidly to a small table near the front door, slid open a drawer, and pulled out an envelope. As she crossed the room with it, Lev Minsky appeared at the bedroom door, yawning. His wrinkled shirt clung to his large, slumped shoulders, his new, very-blue jeans outlined the muscles of his thighs and cinched his soft stomach tightly, so it rolled over the waistband. He watched his wife drop the envelope on the coffee table.

"Eva, already?" he said. "We haven't talked to the woman yet!" Then, to me, as I opened the envelope carefully and slid out the photograph, "I'm sorry to keep you waiting. I was sleeping very soundly."

It was part of a photograph—actually a horizontal section neatly cut off a larger rectangle. The head, bare shoulders and upper chest of a sandy-haired, square-jawed boy. His blue eyes stared angry and scared, lids smudged with illness or exhaustion, dark against the pale cheeks, lips compressed and turned down at the corners. A child on the verge of crying.

The background was solid black; not a clue to his surroundings.

David, I knew, had been missing for three weeks.

"He sleeps too much these days," Eva said. It took me a moment to realize she was talking about Lev. "He's exhausted. We're both exhausted, but I can't sleep at all." Then, "You're a Jew, Ms. Lake?"

"By adoption."

"Lake?"

"It was Lakoff in Russia." Where my father had come from. I was strictly Minnesotan—Chippewa, Swede, and French.

"See, Lev, Russia. And what part?"

"Belarus. A town called Kobrin."

I sat there, patient but claustrophobic, my eyes drawn, over and over again, to that piece of photograph on the table, wanting to turn the conversation back to David. But I was afraid if I didn't allow her this little exercise, this attempt to find a connection, to get some kind of footing in the landslide her life had become, she would suddenly break down and start screaming.

The Minskys were Russian immigrants, in the States only eight months.

"We didn't know any Lakoffs in Moscow, did we, Lev?" He shook his head. "We could have relatives in the United States and never even know it. Names are changed, letters are lost, people die. Sixty, seventy years—a single lifetime—and everything comes undone. Who knew we'd still be running from Europe at the end of the century?" Her voice rose close to the edge of hysteria. Her husband watched her with sad, reddened eyes.

He cleared his throat. "Ms. Lake, can you find our son?"

Eva closed her eyes, and sagged in her chair.

"I don't know. But I can try to. And I'm sure the police are trying as well." The police. Why did the Minskys still have this photograph? Why wasn't it in a police lab, along with its envelope?

He shrugged. "Only someone who can afford to care will find him." Minsky was no fool. There are a lot of lost kids.

"Have the police seen this?" I jabbed my index finger in the direction of the photo.

"No," Lev said.

"Take it to them immediately."

"He even hid it from me for a day," Eva snapped. Then, more gently, "He thinks they'll give it to the newspapers and shame the boy. Or maybe he thinks they won't believe their eyes. Or that they'll blame David."

The postmark showed the envelope had been mailed from Oakland, across the bay, four days back.

"I mean to give it to them," Lev said softly. "It's just hard to part with it."

"Tell me, when exactly did David disappear? What day? What time of day?"

Lev answered, "August seventeenth. A Wednesday. Sometime in the afternoon. He had lunch at home, then went to look at a job with me—the man never showed up. He said he was going home. Around two it must have been. I went to another job site. I was home at four. He never came home."

"Do either of you have any ideas, any theories, about who might have kidnapped him?"

"None," Minsky said with sad finality.

"No one you might suspect who would want to harm your son? Perhaps something happened, an argument, a rivalry—a problem with an adult?"

"We've been in this country eight months," Eva protested. "What could have happened in eight months?"

She might as well have asked me what can happen in eight seconds. Anything. Everything.

"I'll need lists of David's friends. Adults he knows. Friends of yours, people you work with."

"He has plenty of friends," Eva said.

"Even a girlfriend," Lev added.

"Oh, Lev, don't be silly. The boy is only fourteen!" Eva cried.

Lev smiled slightly, the first smile I'd seen. "I think, Ms. Lake, he had a crush. He wrote a poem."

"My husband pinned it to the wall," Eva said, sounding aggrieved, as though the man had crucified her son. "On the wall of his study. I don't know why."

"Why?" He swung abruptly to face her, his high cheekbones inflamed. "I'll tell you why! So I can look at it and not forget what someone has taken away."

I looked at his wife. She was watching him apprehensively. I didn't blame her. I resolved to talk to each of them alone, without the influence or distraction of the other's emotional state.

Minsky glanced at his wife, then back at me. "Eva is searching for craziness," he explained, smiling. "Forget it, Eva. You won't see anything. Not anything but the constant strain of knowing someone is out to hurt us. A mere nothing. Do you want to see the poem?"

Once again, I'd lost the thread, and couldn't immediately remember what he was talking about. Then I nodded.

"Come along, then. I'll show you."

We all three trooped out of the living room and into a tiny room that held a desk and swivel chair, a computer on its own table, an overstuffed chair with ottoman, and a standard lamp.

On the wall above the desk a single sheet of paper was pinned.

I read the poem.

> To Ellen:
> You're beautiful
> and when you smile at me
> I know that I am going to be
> your friend and you will come with me
> and be the girl I love.

* * *

Simple language for a boy his age, I thought. He understood that poetry and obscurity did not have to be the same thing. I wanted to find David Minsky because I wanted to meet him.

I took a manila folder out of my bag. I unpinned the poem and took it down, slipping it into the folder. When I turned around, I found the Minskys both looking at me intently, but with very different expressions. Eva looked expectant, eager, as if she were waiting for me to make a brilliant deduction right then and there. Lev looked outraged.

"Why did you do that?" he demanded.

"I'm going to make a copy of it for my file. Then you can have it back. Why? What's wrong?"

"I suppose nothing," he said, "but you didn't even ask—you simply took it down, as though I had no purpose in putting it there."

Eva had gone past apprehension to embarrassment. But I understood. Emotional, certainly. Eccentric, undoubtedly. But why shouldn't he have a proprietary attitude toward a poem written by his missing child? I'd gotten caught up in the job and forgotten the people. I felt like a fool.

"I'm sorry, that was unthinking and insensitive of me," I said. "But I do want to take it, for a while, anyway. I need to know and understand your son in order to find him."

Lev nodded, his mouth still grudging. "Yes, of course. I'm sorry, too. This is all very hard."

I nodded sympathetically. "The computer. Who uses that?"

"The computer is mine," Eva said. "Donated by a volunteer in Berkeley. I am a computer programmer. My job is, thank God, keeping us alive."

"I work when I can find it," Minsky interjected. "It's not so easy. I'm a structural engineer."

"Easy? Nothing is easy," Eva said. "We come to this crazy country, sacrificing everything, leaving everything we know. He can't find work, and someone steals our child."

"Don't speak against the country that took us in, Eva. Never do that."

Eva shrugged. Obviously, she wasn't so sure. "Forgive me, Ms. Lake, but in Russia, before it changed, you knew where you stood, even if you didn't like where you were standing. Here? Crazy people everywhere. Sometimes I feel like I'm on the wrong side of the planet."

Minsky shook his head. This was obviously a discussion they'd had before.

"It's okay," I said. "You're bound to be disoriented. And you've got every reason in the world to be upset."

I was trying to be reassuring, although the voices of my Chippewa ancestors tended to agree with her: nearly everyone in the U.S. *was* on the wrong side of the planet.

"Did the boy use the computer?"

"Sometimes," Eva answered. "There are probably documents of his in there."

"Will you check?" She said she would. "And Mr. Minsky, will you show me David's room?"

He led me to a small bedroom next to the study, and while Eva began the document search, I began a search of my own. Lev watched me.

The small single bed was neatly made with a plaid bedspread—boys always seem to get plaid bedspreads. Does it have something to do with kilts? A bookcase along one wall was crammed with volumes of all kinds: history, poetry, three dictionaries, several books on baseball, and many, many novels in Russian and in English. An enormous collection of Stephen King. Sheet music. The small desk held a portable typewriter and several notepads filled with writing. The instrument case on the floor beside it contained a brass trumpet.

"I wonder if you could find me a more—characteristic—photo of David? One I can use in my investigation?"

He said he would get me one and left me alone in the room.

I went through the desk drawers. The contents were all a pretty standard-issue fourteen-year-old's, although the yo-yo in the middle drawer might have dated from an earlier time.

Lev came back with a photo. The David in this photo was smiling. He was a stocky, handsome boy with a wide grin, wearing a rugby shirt and jeans, holding an orange cat. I asked him, "Did the police take anything from his room?"

"They looked, but they didn't take anything."

"I will, if that's all right with you." Lev shrugged and sat on the bed. I wasn't used to working with an audience, but he seemed more lonely than distrustful. I went through the boy's books and shook them for odd pieces of paper; I found a few, including several pictures of Madonna. I stuffed everything that seemed relevant into the manila folder with the Ellen poem, and when that was full I slipped papers into my bag. We went back to the living room to wait for Eva.

"Will you be home tomorrow?" I asked.

He nodded.

"I'll call in the morning, come back for the lists."

Eva came out of the study with a floppy disk in her hand.

I took one long last look at the photo that still lay next to its envelope on the coffee table. I studied it, trying to remember it well. I would have to describe it to Tito.

"I'll be in touch tomorrow." I stood.

They both saw me to the door. I walked down the two flights of outdoor stairs to my car, parked on the street, thinking about the boy I was going to try to find. A fourteen-year-old who liked music, baseball, Stephen King, Madonna, an orange cat, and a girl named Ellen. A boy who had now lived in the United States for eight months. If he was still alive.